A Moose on the

Vengeance in Vermont

Bonnie Stock

Moose on the
Roof Books

Vengeance in Vermont
First edition published by Moose on the Roof Books, 2024
Copyright © 2024 Bonnie Stock

Cover design and illustration copyright © Gareth Southwell 2024

ISBN (print): 979-8-9907412-1-8
ISBN (ebook): 979-8-9907412-0-1

This is a work of fiction. Names, characters, places, organisations, incidents, locales, etc, are either the product of the author's imagination, or are used fictitiously. Any resemblance of these fictional elements to actual persons, organisations, etc, is entirely coincidental.

All rights reserved.

No part of this book may be reproduced in any form or by any electronic or mechanical means, including information storage and retrieval systems, without written permission from the author, except for the use of brief quotations in a book review.

To my parents, Caroline and Fisk Hubbell

There is a great deal of wickedness in village life.

– Miss Jane Marple in *The Thirteen Problems*
by Agatha Christie (1932)

chapter one
. . .

THE BODY SHUDDERED ONE final time. There was a rattling groan, then blue-tinged lips pulled back into a gruesome imitation of a smile. Unseeing eyes stared into space until someone drew their hand over them, closing the eyelids forever. Death had come quickly, shocking the small group of onlookers who stood in silent horror, watching the paramedics as they tried in vain to resuscitate the body on the floor. "Cyanotic, non-responsive," the paramedics spoke into their monitor. They both sat back, looking at each other in voiceless acknowledgment that this person's heart had stopped forever. Finally, they quietly packed up their equipment, placed the corpse on a stretcher, and respectfully covered the body with a sheet. They nodded to the assembled group and walked out slowly to the waiting ambulance. There was no hurry. The siren would not be necessary tonight.

The August evening was warm and humid. Moths and midges circled the lanterns by the front door. There was a rustling of small animals – perhaps red foxes or raccoons – in the bushes in the moss-covered graveyard at the back of the building. The former church was now a bookstore. Inside the shop was a quaint café where the group gathered this languid summer night. The warmth of the evening could not dissipate the chilled feeling of the eleven people who huddled together while the paramedics futilely tried to save a life. Moments ago, they were talking and laughing. They were sharing cups of tea and coffee and delicious cupcakes provided by their hosts, the owners of the bookstore. Now, the long farm table was askew, and there were pools of coffee and tea and shards of broken dishes on the well-worn pine floor.

Twelve people gathered here this evening in a small town in southwestern Vermont to discuss a book about death by a local author. The shock was beginning to wear off, and emotions were close to the surface. After all, this had been one of their own, a well-known person in the town of Mill River. Although death was tonight's topic, not one of the remaining attendees thought they would be witnessing it.

Except, perhaps, for the one who caused it to happen.

chapter two
. . .

(ONE YEAR BEFORE)

THE PAINT WAS PEELING, the stained-glass windows were caked with grime, and the two dozen gravestones in the backyard stood silently, marking the years with layers of green mildew obscuring the names of the dead. A solitary black bird perched on the steeple, head cocked, gazing down with one eye at the two people below. The building, erected in 1827 by Congregationalists, was no longer a church but vacant after years of use as a museum, a town hall, and an artist's studio. The couple a hundred feet down on the sidewalk were deep in conversation.

"Emma, this place is right out of a horror movie! You can't be seriously considering it."

He could see his wife viewing the old church with shining eyes and a determined look of anticipation on her face.

"It's perfect, George! This is my bookstore. Moose on the Roof Books."

"Don't you think...?" He wasn't sure what to say.

Emma turned to face her husband. "It's in our price range, it's in the center of town, near a beautiful inn, and other businesses. It'll take some elbow grease, but I can see the potential."

George knew Emma had made up her mind. "Look, let's go have lunch at the little restaurant down the road and talk about it."

He took another look up at the steeple and the graves poking up through the patchy, parched grass and overgrown bushes. The bird was still staring with those dead eyes. George shuddered.

"Come on, sweetheart," Emma said. "A contractor would have this place looking brand new in no time. It has good bones." Turning around once to take in the charming town, Emma hugged George. "This is Vermont. Our dream. It'll be our adventure! How could it be anything but wonderful?"

The sale of the church had gone smoothly, and they were now the proud owners of a rustic old Congregational church. Now, two months later, Emma drove along the two-lane highway singing along with John Denver and the country roads leading home. The winding and hilly road passed under a canopy of maple trees. Most of the branches were bare on this late October morning, but there were still a few brilliant red and gold leaves clinging before dropping to the side of the road, where they would scatter as cars and tractors drove by.

Emma sighed contentedly to herself. "Yes. I am home." Glancing out the window, she noticed houses and barns were decorated with colorful autumn wreaths and Halloween scarecrows. Emma felt a peaceful sense of belonging. After a lifetime on increasingly crowded Long Island, Emma and her husband, George, were thrilled to retire to Vermont. A few more miles down the road, Emma crossed a stone bridge that led her into the small village of Mill River, where the old Congregational Church stood. A church her brilliant local contractor had transformed into Emma's long-held dream, her own bookstore.

This part of southwestern Vermont, known as The Shires, resembled a Grandma Moses painting, with its weather-beaten barns, colorful quilts hung out to dry, church steeples rising into the blue sky, and orchards with fat apples waiting to be plucked. Emma finally reached her destination and parked her brand-new red Jeep, an impulsive retirement gift to herself. Exiting the car, she smiled at a couple of curious passersby and turned her attention to the early nineteenth-century church standing in front of her. The plain exterior was freshly painted white, and the slate gray roof had been patched. The arched front door was now a deep red.

There were two steps leading up to the landing, and Emma placed a large pot of maroon chrysanthemums she had carried from the jeep to the side of the door. She walked back to the sidewalk and turned to look at the building—her very own piece of Vermont! Pleased with the transformation of the exterior, she now envisioned the name of the bookstore over the arch and a welcome sign inviting customers into her new business.

The sky suddenly darkened as a few clouds rolled in, and as Emma looked up, she noticed a large crow perched atop the steeple. She wondered if it was the same bird that spooked George. The creature was glaring down at her as it began squawking. "Calling your buddies to worship?" she called as, one by one, three more crows flew onto the steeple. With thoughts of Alfred Hitchcock swirling in her head, Emma quickly unlocked the front door and entered what had been the sanctuary.

Over the past few weeks, the workers she'd hired had cleared out the detritus that had been accumulating for years. Her contractor refinished the scarred pine floors and painted the walls a crisp white. The stained-glass windows were sparkling, and the crystals from the overhead chandelier cast colorful rainbows on the walls. Best of all, the kitchen, which had been plain and practical, now sported new stainless-steel appliances, a blue-veined granite counter, and sparkling-clean windows. The walls were painted a warm ivory.

She walked to the door leading to the bell tower and knew the small space nestled underneath the stairs would make a perfect private office. She would have to install a good lock on the door so that customers would not explore the stairs and the tower where the bell had once announced the hour of worship. The bell still worked after all these years, but the stairs to reach the tower needed some maintenance. Emma carefully picked her way up to the belfry. Another Hitchcockian moment gave her a flash of vertigo as she discovered that the low wall surrounding the bell had no rail.

She held onto the vertical supports. The steeple afforded a 360-degree view of the quaint town and its surroundings. Across the street was the gray stone Episcopal church with its well-tended yard and ancient graveyard. To the south was a convenience store; beyond that she could see signs for an animal hospital and pharmacy. North of the bookstore were two country inns and a road that led to a covered bridge. She could see the red barns and silos of family farms dotting the autumn landscape.

Although she couldn't see it, she knew there was a family restaurant that had changed hands several times since she and George had fallen in love with the rustic charm of this southwestern corner of Vermont. Beyond that was the stone bridge that spanned the river for which the town was named. The view behind and underneath the steeple was a bit grim. The church had established a small graveyard for a couple of dozen long-dead congregants. It was enclosed by a sharply-pointed wrought iron fence, badly needing repair. The gravestones were green with mildew, and poking up in all different angles, they looked like a mouthful of crooked teeth. She would have to hire landscapers to spruce up the area and clean the stones. The crows she spied perching on the steeple earlier were joined by several others in the unkempt graveyard, happily pecking at some of the bushes.

Emma startled at the sound of a sharp knock on the door. "I'm coming," she called as she stepped carefully down the winding stairway. She smiled in anticipation as she opened the front door, her eyes widening as she gazed at an older man dressed in a severe dark suit with a clerical collar around his neck. "I'm so sorry; I don't mean to stare, but I was just looking at the crows pecking around the graveyard and thinking of Hitchcock movies. Seeing your black suit and collar reminds me of *The Exorcist*." Catching her breath, Emma introduced herself and asked the man, who was actually quite pleasant-looking, to come in.

Laughing good-naturedly, the man extended his hand. "Well, that's an unusual response for sure. But nothing frightening about me, though. I'm Caleb Hill, the minister of the church across the street. I saw the lights on and thought I'd welcome you. As far as the black suit, I'm dressed for a funeral we just held this morning. Just so you're comfortable, I don't do exorcisms."

Emma smiled, happy to meet someone new.

"I've been enjoying watching all the work over here for the past few weeks and wondering what sort of business was moving in," the pastor said, cocking his head in a rather bird-like way. "As far as the crows you've been watching, they may look satanic, but they're just munching on the berries of the juniper bushes the congregation planted years and years ago. You'll find that the birds are intelligent, and they remember people who are kind to them." He took a breath. "Sorry, I'm rambling. Hazard of the job."

Apparently, an expert on the behavior of crows, too, Emma thought. Father Hill was of medium build, a few stray silver hairs combed back from his friendly face and rimless spectacles framed his deep-set blue eyes. "No, nothing frightening about this man," thought Emma. She invited the minister for a cup of coffee in her new kitchen. "This will be my little café," Emma said as she led the clergyman into the kitchen. "I'm hoping that customers will feel comfortable bringing a book back here, pouring a cup of coffee, and having a muffin or cookie." The morning sun poured through the multi-paned windows, throwing a warm glow on the antique pine table. Emma placed two mugs of coffee on coasters with a picture of a moose on them.

As they sat and talked, Emma discovered that Caleb preferred to be called Cal ("Caleb sounds like a character from some book from the 1700s."), and was married to Rebecca, a retired preschool teacher who now played the piano and taught Sunday School.

"It seems to be a requirement that minister's wives play the piano," laughed Cal. "We have three grown children, all scattered across the country. We're now parents of two black labs, a brother and sister from a local shelter."

"Then you would know a good veterinarian," Emma said, sipping her coffee. We have an older cat who will need a checkup soon."

"Oh, Dr Jenkins! He works magic with animals. They love him, as do their owners."

Draining the last of his coffee, Cal said he had some work to finish in his office and invited Emma and her husband to come to church whenever they wished. "Our congregation is small but very welcoming. The door is always open, Emma. Thanks so much for the coffee and the good company. It definitely hit the spot."

Emma extended an open invitation to her bookshop as well.

As the pastor stepped out the door, he suddenly turned back and gave Emma a mischievous grin. "Oh, and Emma. By the way, I am just thinking about your earlier musings. Those birds out in the graveyard? They are called a *murder* of crows." Father Hill waggled his eyebrows and chuckled as he waved goodbye.

"A minister with a dark sense of humor. I like that!" She watched Cal walk across the street and thought she would enjoy getting to know him and his wife. She returned to the kitchen to wash the cups and plates and wipe down the antique pine table she had installed in the kitchen/café. The table and twelve ladderback chairs had been a fortunate find at a barn sale in Manchester. Emma straightened the blue and white woven runner and admired the effect of the table and chairs, which she had outfitted with comfortable matching chair pads.

She strolled out to the main part of the bookstore and envisioned how she would arrange the books she had recently ordered from a wholesaler. Two armchairs with deep cushions were to be delivered over the weekend from Shires Furniture. She would place a coffee table with a pottery lamp between them. The carpenter she hired had built gorgeous pine bookshelves and a matching sales counter. Emma planned to purchase paintings by local artists to grace the empty spots on the walls. There would be an autumn wreath on the door and an antique brass cowbell, given to her by her aunt, to let her know when customers entered the store. She would place a welcome mat on the threshold for people to wipe their muddy or snowy feet. The aromas of coffee brewing and mulled cider simmering on the stove should entice browsers to the cozy café.

Emma's thoughts turned to her husband, George, whom she had left at their small cottage on the outskirts of town. George was diagnosed with Parkinson's Disease a year ago, and she was still nervous about leaving him on his own for more than a few hours. His tremors were still only slight, but recently, he was beginning to see things that weren't there, a possible side effect of the medication he was taking. Most often, he "saw" one of their former cats, an orange tabby named Omar, or his sister, Jennifer, a manager of a Manhattan theater company. This was distressing to both of them, but they had decided to proceed with their planned move to Vermont.

While driving home, Emma passed a few farmstands still selling late-season vegetables, apple pies, jam, and the old paper mill standing astride the river. She turned right onto the maple-shaded lane that led to their cottage and parked on the gravel driveway. When Emma walked through the front door, she nearly tripped over their cat, Annie, who desperately ran into the kitchen. "Ah, so George didn't get around to feeding her," thought Emma. She walked into the kitchen and was startled to see George flat out on the floor. She quickly kneeled by his side and put her hand on his back. "George, are you all right? Did you fall?"

"Oh, stop your worrying," he replied. "I just thought I saw a critter run under the stove, but it seems to have disappeared now."

Knees creaking, George got up slowly, and Emma wondered if this was another hallucination. "Don't you think that Annie would have been tracking it if it were a small animal?" She took her husband's elbow to help him stand.

"I think Annie was intent on her stomach and dinner. You know she's not the sharpest knife in the box."

"Ah, yes," said Emma. "Beautiful but dumb, true. So, I think I'm ready to place the books I ordered on the shelves this weekend. And maybe we can figure out what to do with the landscaping. I'd like to plant some chrysanthemums in front of the store. Do you think you can help me? Oh, and I met the pastor of the church across the street. I think you'll like him."

Emma was chattering on and on when George dropped into his chair at the table, hands on his stomach and feigning hunger. "I'll help, sweetheart. Anything, but do you think Annie and I can have some lunch first? Getting up from the floor took the wind right out of me. Now, what are you fixing us?"

Emma crossed her arms and rolled her eyes at his innocent smile.

chapter three
· · ·

Roger

ROGER MCGARRITY STOOD AT the pharmacy window, looking down the street, as Caleb walked back to his church. The clergyman and a woman he did not know had been standing at the door of the old Congregational Church, talking and laughing. As a business owner in a small town, he was naturally curious about the most recent incarnation of the old church.

"Hey, Dad!" Roger's daughter, Lauren, stood behind him and put her chin playfully on his shoulder. "What are you looking at?"

"I'm just being an old hen, trying to figure out who that woman is and what's happening with the old church." Roger's eyes crinkled as he laughed at himself.

Lauren looked at her father. At seventy, he certainly was getting older but still retained the handsome, rugged good looks of a true Vermont outdoorsman. "Dad, you're just as handsome and fit as you were when you were fifty. And you know, you could take it easy and retire. Your beloved granddaughter is almost done with her studies and will be ready to start learning the business. You should spend more time at the lake—fish to your heart's content. And...I did hear through the grapevine that the woman who bought the church is turning it into a bookstore."

"Glad to hear another business is opening," Roger said. "A bookstore will be good for this town." He turned to his daughter. "So, I have been thinking of cutting back my hours, and Katie could gradually take the helm. But what about you, my dear? You've made a nest out of that office in the back. You are a tremendous manager for the pharmacy, but you can't make it your whole life." Roger gently cradled his daughter's right cheek, his thumb tracing a pink, puckered scar running from her downturned eye to her mouth. "Your mother would have wanted you to have happiness and love in your life."

"Oh, Dad," Lauren sighed, having heard her father's concern many times. "I've learned to be content. I have a couple of friends who accept how I look. I have you and Katie. A good job here. But someone to love, to marry? That's never going to be in the cards for me. That day...those awful boys in high school...took care of that years ago. I won't go through another surgery." Lauren's expression hardened with the memory of that day long ago, which changed her life.

Seeing the sadness in her father's eyes, she quickly recouped, wiped a few stray tears from her eyes, and quickly pecked Roger on the cheek. She noticed a customer coming up the sidewalk and quickly told her dad that she had to get back to work. The bell tinkling over the door interrupted Roger's memory of the accident and its aftermath.

Shaking the cobwebs out of his head, he turned to greet Marie, one of the town's librarians. "Good morning, Marie.

I haven't seen you for a while. I've got to make a trip to the library to stock up on more books." Roger walked with her to the counter, where they continued chatting about their favorite authors, and Roger shared with her the news that a bookstore was taking over the old Congregational Church. Mill River was a small town, and as a pharmacist, Roger knew most of its inhabitants and, in return, was well-loved for his gentle and caring nature. No one would ever suspect that Roger had struggled for years with a hard knot of hatred in his heart.

chapter four

...

ON FRIDAY EVENING, EMMA heard a car pull into the driveway. She peeked out the window and was surprised to see her children, Maggie and Jack, getting out of Jack's old Toyota. Emma threw the door open, called to George, and ran to hug her children.

Emma was thrilled to see her daughter's heart-shaped face and sweet smile. "Hey, Mom! We wanted to surprise you and thought we'd get a look at the bookstore and help with whatever you need. Right, Jack?"

"Oh, sure," said Jack. "But do you have anything to eat? I'm starving!" He doubled over in mock hunger. Her younger child had a bottomless stomach.

Emma laughed as she set them free from her arms. "Come on in, and I'll fix you something."

Emma set some cold cuts, rolls, and fruit on the kitchen table and put on another pot of coffee. They caught up with each other's lives and discussed what still needed to be done at the bookstore. Their conversation lasted until nearly midnight, when, with heavy eyes, they all agreed to get some sleep.

George, however, had wandered off to the couch and nodded off already.

Maggie quietly knocked on the door to her parents' bedroom. "Mom, can I come in?"

"Sure. Is everything okay?"

"I wanted to ask you how Dad really is. Do you think he's up to working at the bookstore with you? What about when he's home alone?"

Maggie and George had developed a special bond early on. He taught her to ride a bike and helped her pick out her first car. When she was home from school because of her frequent sore throats, he came home on lunch hour to play board games or read to her. He was the father she could confide in when she started dating. So, Emma knew how Maggie worried about her dad's new vulnerabilities. "Your dad seems to be doing okay right now. We already have an appointment with a neurologist set up. You know how stubborn he is. He won't give in to Parkinson's without a fight."

Maggie wrapped herself in the soft quilt on the bed. "How is his walking?"

"So far, so good. He's even doing some gardening, clearing out the overgrown weeds and bushes in the backyard." Emma didn't want to mention the episodes of "seeing" one of their former cats or his sister, Jenny. Maggie would find that frightening and worry even more. "I promise I will let you know what the neurologist says. Now, get some sleep. We have some work to do tomorrow...or rather, later today." Emma kissed her daughter on the forehead and hugged her fiercely. "Good night, Mags."

"'Night, Mom."

At the bookstore the next day, Emma gave each person a task. George would shop for coffee, tea, bottled water, butter, and a few different flavors of jam. Maggie and Jack were sent to the nursery to buy colorful chrysanthemums, asters, and a few pumpkins and gourds to place on either side of the front door. Of course, they would have to clear the weed-choked garden along the front of the building. As Jack turned the soil over, Maggie pulled out weeds and planted the flowers. Emma opened the boxes of ordered books and placed them on their appropriate shelves. When George finished shopping, he helped his wife with shelving as well. Finally, they walked out back to the overgrown graveyard and garden.

"Whoa, this is cool! Our parents own a graveyard, Maggie!"

"I know you don't mean any disrespect, Jack. But these graves represent real people who once lived here," said Emma. "Graveyards are sacred places."

Maggie turned to her mother in horror. "Mom, this is scary." Maggie refused to set foot inside the wrought iron fence. "And those birds. Ugh!"

"Don't worry, we won't be working in here. I just wanted to see what has to be done for the landscapers. I think whoever is buried here would like their final resting place to look respectable. Maybe they can clean the graves properly."

The 'murder' of crows simply looked curiously at the group of people standing by the entrance. They soon went back to pecking at the juniper berries.

Glancing at their dirt-stained and dusty work clothes, Emma told everyone to stop and get washed up. "I've made a reservation at the Mill River Inn. We need to celebrate with a special meal."

The Mill River Inn was a stately, historic, 150-year-old inn set back about a hundred yards from the main road running through town. At this time of year, chrysanthemums of several hues adorned the steps and marble path leading up to the double front doors. Pumpkins and gourds spilled from baskets, and white rockers lined the porch. At 6:00, Emma's family sat in the lobby enjoying the warmth from the large stone fireplace while they waited. Emma had requested the table in the cozy nook by the fireplace. The hostess seated them and took their drink orders. After ordering their meal, the inn's owner, June Jamieson, walked over to greet them.

Emma introduced herself and George as the owners of the new bookstore. Emma and June found they had much in common. Both had worked in their pre-retirement years with older folks, June as a nurse in a hospital in Bennington and Emma as a social worker in a nursing home on Long Island. June had grown up in Mill River and was the consummate hostess. When the owners of the Mill River Inn decided to sell and move to a warmer state a few years ago, June and her husband bought the inn and updated it. They now lived in a cottage once used by household staff.

"Emma, let's get together for a cup of coffee when you have a moment," her deep blue eyes twinkling with genuine curiosity. "I'm interested in what you have planned for your bookshop."

"That sounds good," Emma said, excited to have made a new friend. I'll call you soon." The inn was a stone's throw from the bookstore. Emma looked forward to getting to know her new neighbor.

As Emma and her family were leaving, they spotted a gray cat sitting imperiously on the welcome desk. Chrissie, the receptionist, introduced them to Oliver, the inn's resident feline. Oliver took to Jack immediately, rubbing his furry head against Jack's shoulders. Maggie snorted, "Of course, animals just love my brother."

After Emma and George said their goodbyes to Maggie and Jack on Sunday, Emma returned to the bookstore to take an early delivery of the armchairs and coffee table from the furniture store. She placed a pretty pottery reading lamp on the table and a marbled blue vase for flowers. Yesterday, her children had also helped bring her oak rolltop desk into her new office nook. On a table by the door, she displayed some books by her favorite authors, along with local Vermont ones. Intending to make the bookstore warm and homey, Emma decided to visit a few stores in Manchester to purchase prints by local artists, pottery mugs, and autumn accents.

Once Emma was finally done with her shopping, she breathed a sigh of relief. The weekend was at an end, and with Maggie's and Jack's help, they had accomplished quite a lot of work. Emma could think of nothing better than picking up their favorite pizza at Benny's Pizza Restaurant, pouring a couple of glasses of Merlot, and sinking into the couch while she and George put their feet up. Annie snuggled between them as they watched the movie they had selected for the evening, ominously titled The Gathering Storm.

chapter five
. . .

THE BOOKSTORE'S GRAND OPENING would be Thanksgiving weekend. Emma knew she would need a few weeks to relax and take care of other obligations before starting her new business. First on the list was an appointment with Dr Jenkins, the veterinarian Caleb had recommended. She wanted to make sure her thirteen-year-old kitty was in good hands. Dr Jenkins was a charming, fortyish man who seemed to love all four-legged creatures, great and small. Dr Jenkins was tall, and his muscular arms told of his ability to wrangle and treat larger farm animals, such as horses and cows. Emma, however, was taken in by his kind, warm brown eyes.

Dr Jenkins gently lifted Annie out of her carrier, gave her a physical examination, and quickly injected the required vaccines before the cat could cry foul. Emma discovered he had grown up on a dairy farm in Vermont's Northeast Kingdom and now provided care for many of the working animals on local farms. As an avid reader, he looked forward to visiting the bookstore when it opened and asked what the name would be.

Emma laughed and said she had only just ordered the sign but shared that there was a story behind the name.

"Now you have to tell me," the vet said, intrigued. "And, by the way, please call me Rand. We don't stand on much formality around here."

Emma related that years ago, during one of her days home with only her ninety-year-old grandmother, the older woman inched down the stairs and urgently whispered to her granddaughter that a moose was on the roof and looking into her window. Considering this was suburban Long Island, Emma impatiently countered that this was impossible. "I didn't realize that this was the beginning of dementia. I was so young at the time."

"George and I have been vacationing in Vermont for years. Once, we were driving through Bennington and noticed a few businesses had hand-painted, life-size fiberglass moose standing on their rooftops. We broke up in laughter, both thinking that Grandma Hattie had finally been vindicated. Anyway, I've always thought that Moose on the Roof would be a great name for a bookstore, something I've dreamed about for a long time."

"That's a great story," he said as he put Annie back into the carrier. "And your grandma now has her legacy. Good luck with your new venture, and anytime you have a concern about this pretty little cat here, give me a call."

As Emma left the office and put the carrier into her jeep, she thought about her conversation with Rand. She was encouraged that if everyone in town were this welcoming, she would genuinely enjoy becoming part of their community. Emma drove home, murmuring softly to comfort the annoyed cat while enjoying the crisp mountain air. She looked forward to her homemade butternut squash soup for lunch and perhaps a blazing fire in the hearth.

The following morning, after setting Annie's breakfast down and then setting it down again where the fussy cat decided she wanted to eat, Emma and George made oatmeal and coffee for their breakfast. They headed into Bennington to meet Dr Shah, George's new neurologist. They were both surprised to see how young the doctor was. He was also gregarious, intelligent, and informative. The couple were immediately comfortable with him. George patiently answered many questions about his medical history and his initial diagnosis of Parkinson's. Dr Shah then gave him a physical examination and memory test. George's main concerns were stiffness in his legs and occasionally "seeing" a person or animal he knew was not there. The doctor explained changes in perception could happen in some people with Parkinson's, especially after a change in medication. He, therefore, decided not to make any changes to George's current regimen for now. They said their goodbyes to the doctor and his nurse, made a follow-up appointment at the front desk, and headed out into the chilly late morning air.

On the way home, Emma decided to stop at a small grocery store specializing in organic grains, flour, and other unique foods. She enjoyed making her bread and granola and liked supporting local businesses. She bought some oats, dried blueberries, and her favorite maple gouda and couldn't resist the aroma of freshly baked cinnamon raisin bread. When they arrived home, Emma and George enjoyed the bread with butter and a cup of tea. Emma felt it would be a good day to get out of the house, and since George was agreeable, they made plans to eat dinner at the town's most popular family restaurant, The Down Home Grill. Other than the Mill River Inn and a take-out stand, the Grill was the only other option. The restaurant was popular with locals who felt comfortable congregating and sharing news while enjoying home cooking. Emma was also looking forward to meeting her fellow business owners.

Emma put on a pair of gray pants and a light blue sweater. She placed a silver filigree locket George gave her a few Christmases ago around her neck. Standing in front of the full-length mirror in the bedroom, she considered herself. She saw a woman in her early sixties, average height, and weight, with blonde hair streaked with gray and an open face that people seemed to trust. She was also a more substantial woman than she looked and had a steely optimism that her decisions would usually turn out all right, which was how she and George ended up as a retired couple taking on a new venture. The mirror also reflected George getting ready. He was still a nice-looking man with silver hair and a mustache that was perpetually in need of trimming.

Tonight, he wore a pair of khaki slacks with a Fair Isle sweater. Looking at her husband in the mirror, Emma's brow furrowed. She did worry about his diagnosis of Parkinson's and how they would manage if his condition worsened. For now, however, Dr Shah said he was doing well. As promised, Emma would call their daughter later in the evening to let her know the outcome of the appointment. When it was time to leave, they bundled up for the cold Vermont evening, even though The Down Home Grill was only a short distance down the road. They left Annie a snack and, as they always did when they left the house together, called out to her: "Annie, we're going out. You're in charge!"

It was still early in the evening when Emma and George arrived at the restaurant, so only a few of the ten or so tables were occupied. There was a group of men at the bar talking about politics and enjoying some local brews. Emma noticed Rand, the veterinarian, sitting at one of the tables and brought George over to introduce him. "Good to meet you," George greeted the vet. "I hear you were able to charm our Annie."

"She's a sweetie. I think her whiskers are so long you could practically braid them." Rand laughed.

The couple could see Rand was just about to finish his meal, so they said good night and sat where the hostess had directed them. Emma admired the country décor. Old sleds, toboggans, snowshoes, and farm implements hung from the rafters. Paintings by the owner's mother, an artist of some local renown, graced the walls. Emma could see price tags on some of them.

Emma and George had just opened their menus when the front door opened. A heavy-set, ruddy-faced man and his petite wife entered the restaurant. It seemed he already had a few drinks in him as he swayed toward the bar. The man suddenly looked up and glared across the room. Emma realized he was looking at Rand. The man's jaw hardened, and he flushed with anger as he pushed his wife ahead of him into the bar. Rand, visibly uncomfortable, left a wad of bills on the table. With eyes cast down, he walked quickly out the door.

chapter six
• • •

DISTRACTED BY THE TENSE interaction she had just seen, Emma didn't realize the waitress was at their table, pen poised to take their order. "Earth to Emma," George prodded her.

She snapped out of her thoughts. "Oh, I'll have the special, the stuffed delicata squash. And a glass of Chablis, please."

"And I will have the Vermont burger, with cheddar cheese and maple glazed onions," said George, handing both menus to the young waitress.

After the waitress took their order, Emma turned to George and asked if he noticed the couple who had just walked into the bar.

"Sure, the guy looked soused. Pretty wife. Quite a bit younger."

"Yes, and the wife looked like she'd rather be anywhere but here. Did you see her stiffen when her husband pushed her toward the bar? I wonder who they are. The guy gave a killer look to Rand."

"I do not doubt that you will find out, Emma."

Their meals arrived, and their attention turned to the delicious food in front of them. As Emma sipped her white wine, she noticed the chef stirring a large pot in the kitchen. His body language conveyed the sense that he was at home behind his stove. He was a large, muscular man, and Emma could see a tattoo peeking out from his chef's apron. The woman beside him adding slices of tomato to the pot was "earthy," Emma concluded. She was broad in the hips and shoulders and had a long braid trailing down her back, wisps of chestnut hair escaping wildly in the steam. Emma assumed she was the chef's wife from how they worked together.

George could see his wife's thoughts meandering as they often did while observing people. "Emma, do you want coffee and dessert?"

"I'm full. We can make some coffee at home, and we always have ice cream. I still have to call Maggie."

They called the waitress for the bill and walked over to the old-fashioned cash register at the bar. The woman Emma had seen in the kitchen came over to take their check, and Emma remarked how wonderful the dinner was.

"I'm sure glad to hear it. Are you two seeing the sights in Vermont? You sort of missed the high season for leaves." The woman was tall and solidly built. Her cheeks were flushed pink from working in the kitchen, and she smiled easily. Emma thought she could be described as wholesome rather than pretty.

"Actually, we live down the road and heard this was the place for a good, home-cooked meal," replied George congenially.

"Well, a big welcome to you all. I'm Janie, and my husband Mike and I bought up this place a year or so ago. Mike's lived here all his life, but I'm a little out of my element coming from the South."

"I can hear that twang in your voice," George said. "You two seem to be doing very well here." He indicated that the dining room had been filled since their arrival. "My burger was delicious."

"Thanks, sir. We really enjoy it here, and I do hope you'll come back soon."

Emma saw Janie's eyes glancing over to the corner table where the couple who walked in earlier now sat. Hoping to extend the conversation, Emma piped up. "I think we'll see you often." She explained about the bookstore and introduced herself and her husband.

Janie slammed the cash register as she regarded Emma. "Yeah, I did hear someone bought that old place. Lots of bookstores sell food. Will you be doing that too?" She crossed her arms, her brow wrinkled in a frown, and her smile faded.

"Just coffee and some cake or muffins," Emma answered, wariness creeping into her voice.

"Mmm, okay," Janie said as she stepped back from the register. Good luck to you." She took one more concerned look at the corner table. "Listen, I think Mike needs me in the kitchen. Take care." And just like that, the conversation came to a chilly and abrupt halt, confusing Emma and George after the beginning of an otherwise friendly chat.

After Emma called Maggie and reassured her that all was well, Emma got ready for bed, wondering what had caused Janie's abrupt change in demeanor. She also thought about the pretty young woman whose husband radiated anger. Emma knew, realistically, there was no such thing as an ideal place to live. Tremors would always simmer under the surface, nasty or quirky personalities populating the town, with troubles she had yet to discover.

As the owner of a brand-new business and hoping to fit into Mill River, Emma resolved to understand her new town and the people who would either enhance or complicate their lives. Tomorrow, she would call June at the Mill River Inn and invite her for a cup of coffee and conversation. It was time to understand more about the town she now called home.

chapter seven

· · ·

RAND

RAND DROVE HOME CAREFULLY from the Down Home Grill. He was still unnerved by Walter's behavior this evening. He parked in the driveway. As he entered his comfortable farmhouse, he was greeted enthusiastically by Red, his golden retriever, and Skittles, the calico Maine Coon he'd rescued from nearby Another Chance Animal Center. After giving his beloved pets hugs and snacks, Rand poured a couple of fingers of brandy into a mug and sat down in his leather recliner. With Red stretched out by the side of the chair and Skittles settling into his lap, Rand sighed with contentment at the love his companions showed him. Taking a sip of his brandy, he thought about the scene at the restaurant.

Walter was already drunk and ready to pick a fight. Although Walter's eyes were focused on him, Rand found and locked onto Grace's eyes. He was shocked by the resignation he saw in them. As a veterinarian, Rand worked closely with Grace and Walter, caring for their dairy farm's working and domestic animals. Always suspicious of his wife's working relationship with men, Walter had recently...and correctly...sensed more of a connection between Grace and Rand.

Grace loved her horses and cows. To her, they were family, not just working creatures. Rand admired that attitude. It didn't hurt that Grace was pretty and sensitive. They fell into a rhythm working together and enjoyed talking about books, family, and the news. Walter discovered them side by side in the barn, looking too cozy. He fired Rand on the spot and threatened him with bodily harm if he ever saw him with Grace again.

Rand gently put the sleeping cat on the floor, where she curled up next to the lab. Red settled himself more comfortably around Skittles, and Rand chuckled as he listened to the purrs and snores of his two furry friends. The veterinarian walked onto the front porch and sat on the steps, looking at the stars twinkling in the clear autumn sky. At moments like this, gazing up at the vast sky and feeling so insignificant, he realized he was lonely.

He and his wife finalized their divorce a year ago. Hailey had heard the rumors of a blossoming friendship between her husband and Grace and confronted him about it. Counseling had not worked. She simply moved on. It happened so fast it made Rand's head spin. Red and Skittles provided much-needed companionship, but he missed a woman in his life. A woman like Grace.

He had come to know Walter well during the time he treated his farm animals. Walter was bright and could be charming. He could also be mean, especially after a few drinks. Rand fervently hoped the farmer would refrain from taking out his spite and anger on Grace and their children tonight. Although Grace would try to protect her son and the two younger girls, Walter could easily overpower his petite wife. In contrast to Walter, Rand was proud of his gentle demeanor and the professional standing he enjoyed in Mill River. He thought of the damage a vengeful Walter could do to his reputation. Rand was surprised as he looked down. His fists were clenched in anger, a rare feeling for the town's beloved veterinarian.

chapter eight
. . .

AFTER BREAKFAST THE FOLLOWING morning, Emma and June made plans to meet at the bookstore that afternoon between lunch and dinner at the Inn.

"George, I'm leaving now," Emma said. "There's soup in the fridge you can heat up for lunch and some fresh rolls, too. Don't forget to feed Annie. I'll be back as soon as I can." She walked out into another blustery day, with predictions of snow flurries that evening. She was well-bundled up in a puffy jacket and wool scarf. Her first stop was the pharmacy to pick up the medication Dr Shah had renewed. She liked Roger immediately. He typified a Vermont outdoorsman with his jeans, obligatory plaid flannel shirt, and well-worn boots underneath his pharmacist's coat. He had a full head of salt and pepper hair and a quick smile.

"I hear you're the new bookstore owner down the road. I hope you do well."

Just then, a young woman with a serious demeanor stepped to the counter next to Roger. She wore a pharmacist coat as well and extended her hand in greeting. "I'd like to introduce my granddaughter, Katie. We're training her to take over the business."

"I'm pleased to meet you. I hope to see you both at the bookstore when it opens."

"We're delighted that another business is coming to town. We will definitely be customers." Katie had shiny, dark, shoulder-length hair and an intelligent look in her blue eyes.

Always in "mother mode," Emma thought about how she would like to introduce this lovely young woman to Jack. Emma noticed another woman working on a computer behind a glass partition. The woman had not turned around, and Emma wondered why she hadn't looked up. Most people were friendly and liked to chat with a newcomer. She shook off the thought as she returned to her car and headed up the hill toward the town's library.

Emma had never seen such a small library—the size of a one-room schoolhouse—but the two librarians seemed to work together well. They hoped the town's revitalization plans would include improving their facility to serve more of the community's residents and add to their staff. Emma got a new library card.

"I know this is a bit forward, but once you get settled, can we talk about holding some programs at your store?" one of the librarians, Caroline, asked. "We're so small here that it's difficult, and we must restrict the group size." Caroline appeared to be a warm, maternal woman. She peered at Emma over rimless glasses perched on the tip of her nose.

"Certainly, once I'm up and running." Emma realized working with the librarians could only benefit the library and her store. "In the meantime, I hope you'll come see us. I'm quite proud of how the bookstore looks."

Driving back down the hill to the bookstore, Emma smiled, thinking about the people she had met that day. However, she could not keep her thoughts from returning to the scene at The Down Home Grill and was anxious to ask June about it. Once she arrived at the bookstore, Emma put on a pot of coffee and set out a couple of lemon blueberry muffins.

A few minutes later, June was at the door, and the two women greeted each other with a hug. June was dressed casually in jeans and a blue chambray shirt, her brown hair styled in a short bob. June's no-nonsense manner told of her years of nursing. After chatting about their day, their husbands and family, and, of course, the always-variable Vermont weather, Emma put her elbows on the table, leaned forward, and gave June an earnest expression. "I need to know a little about the people I will be dealing with in town. I love it here and want to make a go of my business and become part of the community. I do know that might be hard for an outsider. I've met some wonderful people, but George and I had dinner at the Grill last night, and I had my first taste of another side of life here."

June arched her eyebrows inquisitively, sipped her coffee, and broke off a piece of her muffin. "Ugh! I shouldn't have this. I've been trying to lose five pounds forever."

"It's always the last few pounds that do us in, right? Anyway, a couple walked in shortly after we sat down. The man was heavy-set but strong-looking, and I'm assuming the woman with him was his wife. She was petite, had long reddish-blonde hair, and truly seemed uncomfortable. It seemed like he had been drinking. I noticed he looked daggers at Rand, who was seated by himself. Rand was out the door not a minute later." Emma cocked her head to the side, frowning in consternation. "Then, when the chef's wife took our check, we were having a nice conversation until she found out we were opening the bookshop and offering coffee and cake. Then, she seemed just to shut down. Any idea what's going on?"

June wrapped her hands around her mug and leaned back in her chair. "I'm sure I know who the couple was at the Grill, and I know Janie and Mike. We've got our share of interesting people and intertwined relationships. Most of what I tell you is an open secret, and some my speculation. But it is a small town, and you will need to work with these people, so this is my take." June took a sip of her coffee and, with a reflective look in her eyes, began her story.

chapter nine
...

"THE COUPLE YOU SAW coming into the restaurant must be Walter and Grace Eammons—their dairy farm's outside of town. Rand had been their veterinarian. Between well-care and calf birthing, Rand spent a fair amount of time on the farm, primarily with Grace. She oversees the animals while Walter runs the business and brings in customers. Grace is devoted to her animals and treats them like members of the family. In their case, you could say that Rand and Grace bonded over the cows, maybe a bit too much bonding. Walter sensed something brewing and threw Rand out on his nice little you-know-what!" June laughed at her comment. "I will admit to admiring that man."

"Rand was married. Hailey was also a veterinarian and was unhappy about Rand's spending so much time with Grace. The marriage was troubled even before that came to light. She initiated a divorce, moved up north, and works for a large veterinary clinic."

"You've lived here all your life," Emma said. "Did you know Walter?"

"Sure did. I've known him since he was a kid growing up on his parent's farm. He took that over when his parents retired. Walt's always been full of contradictions." June put her mug down, and put one hand out, palm up. "On one hand, he seems like a good ole' boy, enjoying a few drinks – or maybe more than a few – with the local guys. He can be aggressive and has a temper." She held the other hand up. "On the other hand, he's a farmer with an excellent education, a degree in animal science." June put her hands down and took a sip from the coffee mug. "He knows his business and has been more successful than his parents ever were. His family goes way back to the Revolutionary War, ancestors in local graveyards, and all that history that he loves to jabber on about. I have a feeling he will be a good customer at the bookstore."

"He seemed awfully threatening to me. I can see that he could throw his weight around. What about his wife, Grace? She seemed mortified at the restaurant."

"She's a nice person, maybe a little naïve. Grace is a few years younger than Walt. I think whatever love they had to start with has faded. But they do have three kids, the oldest of whom is in junior high. I don't think Grace can or would ever leave. She'd be terrified of what Walter would do." June added that her husband, Rob, was once a psychology professor who had a clinical practice. "His take on Walter is that he is a classic narcissist. "We have no idea if he is physically abusive to Grace, but we've heard him berate her in public. Not that I've seen any evidence, but I would not be surprised if he has begun to escalate."

Emma wondered how Rand managed to live and work in a town with gossip about his alleged relationship with Grace hanging over his head.

"He keeps his nose to the grindstone, is a great vet, and a good man," replied June. "It's pretty clear he cares about Grace, and I'm sure he feels awful that Grace is bearing the brunt of Walter's anger."

Emma took a sip of her coffee and wrinkled her nose. "Ugh! Cold. Do you want a refill?"

"No, I need to get back to the Inn, but let's talk quickly about Janie's reaction when you paid your check."

"Sure. I feel awkward about returning. It almost seemed like she thought I'd be stealing her customers."

Finishing her muffin, June wiped her mouth with her napkin and nodded affirmatively. "You're probably right. You're a new business that will offer a place for customers to hang out with a cup of coffee and a snack. This is a town that has seen its share of businesses go under. We depend on the weather for tourists, and it has been unpredictable for a few years. Janie apparently grew up poor. She may feel threatened."

"I have an idea that may help," June said, offering advice. "If you're going to serve muffins, scones, and the like, you might consider asking Janie to cater. She is an incredible baker. She also preserves jam and sells it at the farmer's market on Saturday mornings. We serve a nice breakfast at the Inn, but you haven't tasted anything as wonderful as Janie's cornmeal pancakes and homemade sausage. Janie grew up in Appalachia and brings her Southern roots into everything she makes. I think turning her into an ally would benefit both of you."

"June, that is an amazing idea. Thank you! And Janie's husband, Mike? What's he like besides being a great chef?"

"Nice guy. Uncomplicated. Born and bred Vermonter, happiest behind the stove with a wooden spoon or spatula in his hand. I think he met Janie on a fishing trip to West Virginia with some of his buddies. They seem really in tune with each other. Neither of them has any use for Walter, except as a customer, but they love Grace and would do anything for her."

June stood up and reached for her jacket. "Emma, I love what you've done to this old place. So cute. If you get business cards made up, give me some, and I'll put them at the reception desk at the inn."

Emma realized it was later than she thought when she said goodbye to June. She quickly washed the dishes, turned the heat down, and the lights off. She bundled into her coat, scarf, and gloves, hurried to the car, and drove home through snow flurries, leaving the outside lantern on. She apologized to George for leaving him so long, but he had happily been reading all afternoon. They made a simple dinner of scrambled eggs, toast, and fruit salad and watched the early news. Emma told her husband all that June had shared with her that afternoon.

He agreed that asking Janie to bake for the bookstore was a good idea. In his private thoughts, however, he worried that Walter would prove to be a problem at the bookstore, and given Janie's insecurity, whether she would ever accept that other businesses did not need to threaten hers. He and Emma were now invested in this town and creating a thriving business. He knew his wife tended to see the best in people; her nature was to "fix" them and their problems. As an ex-cop, George knew life could get ugly and that people who felt angry or threatened did not often change.

chapter ten

...

PRECISELY AT SEVEN A.m. on the Saturday before Thanksgiving, Annie jumped onto the bed and plopped down on Emma's chest, whiskers tickling Emma's nose.

"Oof! Okay, Okay, I got the message. Let's get you some breakfast. You get to snooze while we have a full day planned!" Yawning and stretching, Emma got out of bed and shuffled to the kitchen. She spooned some cat food into a dish, placed it on the floor, gave the cat fresh water, and set the table for breakfast – homemade granola, milk, bananas, and coffee. George smelled the aroma of the coffee and joined his wife in the kitchen. As they sat looking out the window at the cardinals and chickadees at the bird feeder, Emma took out her to-do list for the day. George groaned good-naturedly when he saw the list, but he knew Emma would go gentle on him. Still, the errands would get done.

An hour later, jackets and gloves on with car heater blasting, Emma and George drove north to a small town that hosted a farmer's market every Saturday. One of the larger and more popular markets, it was held at the village Grange

Hall. The parking lot was packed even at this early hour, owing to tourists and locals enjoying the variety of available goods. Entering the market, Emma took out her list and encouraged George to browse to his heart's content. He happily went off in search of a Christmas gift for Emma. Not only were there baskets of fall vegetables, apples, artisanal cheeses, loaves of bread, jams, and maple syrup products, there were vendors selling jewelry and rustic crafts.

Emma walked through the crowd toward the table of her favorite cheese makers. She selected several, which she planned to serve at the bookstore's grand opening party. She walked away with a bag laden with smoked maple gouda, goat cheese, creamy bleu cheese, and a sharp Vermont cheddar.

Her next stops were to purchase hummus from a local bakery (and a crusty multigrain for herself and George) and a couple of bottles of wine from one of the new Vermont vineyards. She would buy champagne, chips, and crackers at the grocery store nearby. As Emma scouted the market for George, she noticed Janie sitting in one of the corner booths talking with a customer. As June had mentioned, she offered a selection of her homemade jams. After the customer left, Emma summoned her courage, walked over to the table, and greeted her. The younger woman hesitated slightly but, with a lift of her chin, stood and greeted Emma. "I heard you sold your jam at the farmer's market, and well, here you are." Emma cringed at how formal she sounded. "I've heard you're a talented baker as well."

"Um, yeah, actually, I had some Morning Glory muffins on the table, but they're all sold out. Are you interested in any jam? I put up some blueberry and strawberry rhubarb this summer."

"Sure, we love strawberry rhubarb. I'll be happy to take one of those." Emma also asked about the bottles of dried herbs she saw on the table. Janie explained that as a child growing up in Appalachia, her grandmother had taught her all about the benefits and dangers of herbs, and now she grew her own, as well as foraged in the woods. As Janie handed her the jar of jam she had purchased, Emma took a deep breath. "Janie, what would you think about baking for the bookstore? I can't do it all myself and want to offer homemade cookies and muffins."

Emma could see that Janie was trying to weigh her response. "I'll talk to Mike. We bake every day for the restaurant, so I suppose I could probably add a dozen or so more, but I'll have to let you know. That all right with you?"

"Sure. We'll talk after we open next week. Figure out what you'd charge, all right? Well, enjoy your Thanksgiving, Janie." Emma thought it was a bit of a stilted conversation, but she hoped that Janie would accept her as just another customer, not as competition.

Emma found George over by the "potato lady," as he always called her. She sold several unique varieties of potatoes, and he could never resist buying a pound of German butterball or purple fingerling from this knowledgeable and kind woman. After shopping at the market, they returned to the jeep and drove back to town for the rest of their errands. The first stop was the sign maker. Smiling at the logo, Emma couldn't wait until it was installed over the shop's door. The rest of their errands were accomplished relatively quickly, including getting a turkey and trimmings for Thanksgiving dinner. They stopped at a farm stand to order apple and pumpkin pies.

They were finally home by mid-afternoon. While Emma put everything away and fed Annie, George sat at the kitchen table, catching his breath. He found that he tired more quickly these days. Afterward, he lit a fire in the hearth. Emma assembled an early dinner of tomato basil soup and chunks of multi-grain bread with sharp cheddar and a sliced apple. Feet warming in front of the fire, they cuddled with a purring Annie, content with a full stomach. Emma was too tired to think of Janie for the rest of the evening.

At the farmer's market, she had not seen Grace walk over to Janie's table to bring her a cup of coffee and to share the latest altercation with her husband. Grace appreciated that her friend was always available to commiserate with her. What she didn't understand was that Janie felt Grace's pain in a profoundly personal way.

chapter eleven
...

JANIE

WHEN JANIE RETURNED TO the restaurant that afternoon, she found her husband, Mike, working on that evening's special: pork chops with roasted onions and apples and a vegetarian offering of acorn squash stuffed with quinoa, dried fruit, and walnuts. She leaned against the counter to watch Mike skillfully chop and slice the vegetables and fruit.

"Hey, Janie," he said, leaning over to kiss her absentmindedly on the cheek. "How was the market today?"

"Good. Just about everything sold out. Lots of out-of-towners today."

"That's great." Mike took a moment to look at his wife. So why the long face? Did something happen?"

"You know that lady who bought the old Congregational church? I told you she's making it into a bookstore, right? Also, serving coffee and muffins and stuff? Well, she asked me if I was interested in baking for her a few days a week."

"So, the problem is...?"

"Mike, what if she takes our business away? I don't want to help her do it!"

Mike tried to relieve his wife's look of anguish. "You worry too much. A bookstore selling a few cups of coffee and some muffins will not affect us. We have our regular customers. And maybe her bookstore will bring more people to town who will have lunch or dinner here. Hey, ask her if she can display some of our cards."

"Well, what if I don't want to share, Mr Optimism? I'll have to think about it," Janie pouted. "Grace came by too. I swear, that man'll be the death of her. After they left here the other night, Walter couldn't wait to get home to dress her down just because Rand had the nerve to be in the same place at the same time. Grace said he was having trouble getting the key in the lock – too much hooch, you know – and when she tried to help him, he pushed her away. Hard. She hurt her hand breaking her fall. Mike, she needs to get away from him!"

"Sweetie, you're a good friend, but you need to be careful giving advice to Grace."

Janie laid her head on Mike's shoulder, feeling his warmth and strength. "I know, but not everyone is as lucky as I got. How did I ever deserve you?"

"You got that right, my darlin'." Mike planted another kiss on Janie's head and shooed her away. "Now, let me finish up here. Can you set up in the dining room? My mom's running late."

Grumpily, Janie grabbed some silverware, napkins, and salt and pepper shakers from the sideboard and began setting up the tables. She was not, however, in the mood to be placated. Mike didn't understand, she thought. He grew up in a loving, stable home. A home where a wife didn't have to watch her husband's moods, children felt safe, and had few financial worries. "Nothing like my home," Janie muttered under her breath.

chapter twelve

...

ON THANKSGIVING EVE, MAGGIE and Jack arrived at the cottage. On their drive north, they stopped in Manhattan to pick up Jennifer, George's sister, the manager of a theater company. The cottage suddenly seemed smaller with three additional people bustling in, carrying baggage and offerings for the holiday feast. It was, however, warm and welcoming, with the aroma of cranberries and oranges simmering on the kitchen stove and the spicy scent of candles placed strategically around the cottage. Maggie and Jennifer stored their suitcases in the guest room, and Jack brought his up to the small loft bedroom.

Afterward, everyone settled down in the living room for drinks and snacks. They talked about their jobs and Jennifer's latest stage production. They listened as Emma and George shared all they discovered about Mill River, the people they met, and their plans for Friday afternoon's bookshop's grand opening party.

Emma woke up early on Thanksgiving morning and, with Maggie's and Jennifer's help, finished preparing the turkey, stuffing, and other side dishes. George and Jack set the table, poured drinks, set out the appetizers, and brought in more wood for the fireplace. By late afternoon, the family was ready for their traditional Thanksgiving dinner. George offered the grace, and Jennifer made a toast. The dishes were passed around, and the family heartily enjoyed the food.

"Mmm, Mom, you made my favorite sweet potato casserole," exclaimed Maggie.

Jack could only nod in appreciation; he was so busy eating. Emma, as always, looked around the table, grateful for her wonderful family. She could not help but think about the people who were no longer with them and whom she missed dearly. She wondered how the Thanksgiving meal at the Episcopal Church turned out. She had contributed her signature holiday dish, the candied sweet potato casserole and homemade cranberry sauce. Father Cal and Rebecca hosted dinner in the church's basement for those in town who could not afford a meal or had nowhere to go. Members of the church were generous in their contributions of food, and a few volunteered their time to serve.

Elsewhere in Mill River, other town residents celebrated Thanksgiving, some happily, and others hoped some of that holiday joy could be theirs. Rand was spending his first Thanksgiving alone since his divorce. He wanted to feel useful and to be with people, so he volunteered to help serve the meals at the church. After all the guests were served, he and the other volunteers enjoyed their plates full of turkey, apple, and pumpkin pies for dessert. Rand helped to clear the tables and wash the dishes before going home.

He brought a few leftovers for Red and Skittles, who sniffed turkey and immediately circled his legs, impatiently waiting for handouts. Rand settled in front of the television set with a can of beer. At least there was football to keep his mind occupied. Unable to sit still, he paced, looking out his windows, and ending up on the porch, he looked up at the orange-hued Harvest moon. His mind was turning to Grace and Walter and their family meal. Were they finishing up now? Were Walter and his brother drinking? Rand knew that holiday dinners and football were excuses to drink to excess, making Walter mean. He hoped Grace and her children would be spared from Walter's temper this evening.

In fact, the Eammons family was just finishing their dessert. "Yum, Mom. The best apple pie ever!" their middle-schooler, Jesse, said. "Can we be excused, please?" The three kids absconded quickly to play video games in Jesse's bedroom. Walter and his brother retrieved another six-pack from the refrigerator and sat in the living room to watch the last game of the night. The men were already two sheets to the wind when Grace, clearing the table, accidentally dropped a wine glass. She stiffened immediately as it shattered noisily, with dregs of wine spilled on the hardwood floor.

Walter lifted his large body from the armchair and stumbled into the dining room. "You clumsy bitch! That was one of my grandmother's glasses. Just...clean this mess up!" He had approached Grace belligerently, and Grace backed into the kitchen to retrieve a mop, pan, and broom to sweep up the jagged shards. On her knees, with Walter looming drunkenly nearby, Grace kept her head down and prayed that her children hadn't heard his outburst.

"How can my life have come to this?" Grace thought. She picked up a large shard of glass and imagined what she could do with it. She slipped it into her pocket while Walter was focused on the game and hid it in the back of a kitchen drawer. It would be there for protection if needed. Walter had always lashed out verbally, but recently he had begun to shove her when he was angry, which happened more often now. "What would happen if I stood up to him?" Grace thought. She knew if not for her children, she would have left him. Was a good life still possible? All Grace ever wanted was a family, a home, and the feeling of security.

At The Down Home Grill, Janie, Mike, and Mike's mother, Ronnie, were sending their staff home from the restaurant. They'd held an afternoon seating for their customers on this holiday. They were about to sit down to turkey, glazed ham, chestnut stuffing, mashed potatoes, bush beans and carrots preserved from Janie's garden, and her homemade cranberry pecan pie. In their small home next to the restaurant, Ronnie set an artistic table and lit some tapers, and Mike and Janie brought the dishes into the dining room.

After serving others all day and then clearing up the kitchen, they dug in without fanfare. Sated, Janie closed her eyes and said a silent prayer of thanks for these wonderful people who had welcomed her into their family. There was never a holiday dinner in her tiny West Virginia town that did not end with drunken anger and recriminations. Although Janie's grandmother provided a stabilizing presence in her life, she died when Janie was twelve, leaving the young girl feeling more alone than ever. Janie's parents fought bitterly. Her mother earned a small but steady income as a waitress in the town diner. Her flirty interactions with male customers, though, led Janie's father to lash out in jealous tirades fueled by alcohol. Darrel was clever, though. He only left bruises where they couldn't be seen.

Guiltily, Janie wished her father was dead or that her mother would wake up and leave. Meeting and marrying Mike quieted most of her fears and anxieties. She felt secure with her husband most of the time in this beautiful and tranquil Vermont town. Alone with her thoughts, however, Janie could not shake the feeling that her peaceful life could be shattered at any moment.

At the Mill River Inn, June and Rob Jamieson and their family celebrated Thanksgiving dinner after their last guests departed the dining room. Their youngest grandchild had been put to bed, and the adults and older grandchildren enjoyed the delicious meal the Inn's chef had left for them. They caught up on each other's lives and felt blessed to gather in this charming, historic country inn. June told her family about the new bookshop opening this weekend and the friendship that had begun to blossom with the owner, Emma Nielsen. The three Jamieson children agreed they would like to visit the store on Saturday and stock up on Christmas presents. Across the table, June and Rob shared a smile, both feeling so fortunate to have a family who loved one another and were willing to reach out to others to help them thrive as well.

Pharmacist Roger McGarrity sat down to dinner with his daughter and granddaughter in his new log cabin nestled by a lake in the Green Mountains. They had been hiking through the snowy woods surrounding the cabin, observing deer, fox, and the wild turkeys who had escaped being on today's menu. Roger was thrilled to see Lauren red-cheeked and laughing as they chased his King Charles Spaniel through the snow.

"Charlie," Roger called. "Come back here now." There was always a chance of running into a moose, and Charlie was no match for such a creature.

"How about heading back, Dad?" Lauren called, waiting for Roger to catch up. "Katie and I are freezing and hungry!"

"Yup, let's go! We've got a feast waiting to put on the table." He took a sidelong glance at Lauren and noticed the cold air had made her scar bright red. But being with her family in the woods and fresh air had lightened her spirits, and Roger's heart swelled for her. When they returned to the cozy cabin, they poured glasses of Cabernet Sauvignon and set out a plate of sharp cheddar and crackers while they waited for the turkey to finish browning.

After the Thanksgiving meal at the church, Father Cal and Rebecca walked back to the parsonage hand in hand, the icy snow crunching beneath their feet. This was their first time hosting a meal at the church, and their hearts were warmed by the food lovingly provided by the volunteers and the spirit of thanks from those who needed a good meal. At the parsonage, the couple put on a pot of tea and sat down to the pieces of pie they were too busy to eat before. "I couldn't eat one morsel more," said Caleb as he leaned back in his chair, hands over his protruding stomach.

"Well, I'm going to call the kids. I missed them this year, but I know traveling over the holidays is expensive. Maybe we could visit one or two of them over the summer, dear?"

"Absolutely. And maybe one of them will bring their family for Christmas. There isn't anything like Christmas in Vermont."

Emma's new acquaintances, the town's librarians, spent the holiday dinner with family and friends. The library would open late tomorrow, but they knew it would not be busy. Black Friday was still the traditional start to Christmas shopping. Caroline and Marie were both looking forward to seeing the new bookstore. They were invited to the grand opening party the next afternoon, along with a few other people the new owners had met.

No one in the small town of Mill River, whether sharing a Thanksgiving dinner with family or friends, hiking through the woods, watching a football game, or picking up shards of shattered glass, could know that opening a country bookstore would set into motion a series of events that would threaten the placidity of this community and its inhabitants.

chapter thirteen
. . .

EMMA AWOKE THE MORNING after Thanksgiving with a fluttering in her chest. "Please just be anxiety. I don't need a heart attack today," she prayed. "George, George, wake up!"

"Emma, we don't have to be at the bookstore for hours," George groaned. Everything is set. The refreshments are already there, and the champagne is chilled. Ed will bring the sign over on time. Just take a breath."

Emma and George put on their bathrobes and walked into the kitchen. They were pleased to see that Jennifer had the coffee perking. Jennifer's long brown hair, increasingly laced with silver, was up in curlers.

"Good morning!" George's sister sang. "It's your debut today." She laughed as she poured three mugs of coffee.

It always warmed Emma's heart to take in Jennifer's cheerfulness, wide-open smile, and big blue eyes. Jennifer was as tall as her brother and had the broad shoulders of an athletic swimmer. She still swam in amateur races at the YMCA, but her heart belonged to the theater. They took their coffee mugs to the kitchen table. Emma set out placemats and put homemade farmer's bread, butter, and Janie's strawberry rhubarb jam in the center of the table. Annie sauntered in, demanding her breakfast too. The house slowly came to life, with Maggie and Jack joining them at the table and bringing out cereal and bananas.

After breakfast, Emma reviewed some last-minute plans for the day's festivities before everyone retreated to their rooms to get ready. Emma showered and dressed in her heather blue wool dress, draping a matching shawl around her shoulders and adding tights and lined boots for warmth. She slipped a necklace that had been her mother's around her neck. The heart-shaped locket contained photos of Maggie and Jack when they were toddlers. Emma considered this her "good luck" talisman.

Once again, she looked into the full-length mirror and breathed deeply. "Well, this is it, the make-or-break moment." Emma planned to leave earlier than everyone else to turn on the heat, put out the refreshments, and ready the coffee pot and tea kettle. She was expecting her sign aficionado, Ed, an hour earlier than the guests she had invited, and she wanted to make sure her nerves were calm.

A few minutes later, Emma greeted Ed as he pulled up in front of the store with her long-awaited sign. He brought a ladder and tools from his truck and got to work. Emma stood back, gazing up at the sign. "Ed, you're an artist. Thank you for bringing my vision to life."

Ed placed a tarp over the sign so that it could be revealed at the ribbon-cutting ceremony. An hour later, a small group had assembled in front of the bookstore. In addition to Emma's family, she had invited her new friends, the Jamiesons, Rand,

Roger, Caleb and Rebecca, and Caroline and Marie. The head of the town council was there and had brought along a photographer to record the opening of a new business.

Jack and Maggie held a red ribbon across the doorway, and the guests cheered as Emma and George cut the ribbon together. Ed dramatically ripped away the tarp covering the sign, and everyone clapped and smiled as they saw it. Moose on the Roof Books, written in gold lettering, featured green mountains in the background and a moose proudly standing atop the steeple of the old church, now a bookstore. Ed's face fairly glowed after receiving so many compliments.

After everyone filed into the store, Emma and George ensured they all held a glass of champagne as they toasted the small town's newest business. Emma had to explain how she came to name the bookshop to the town councilman and Roger, who had not heard the story of her grandmother and the moose. It was a congenial group who had gathered to congratulate the Nielsens and wish them well.

Emma was in the cafe pouring the coffee and tea into carafes and arranging the cookies on a plate when she heard a door slam, and the laughter and chatter in the next room abruptly stopped. She peeked out of the café's door and saw the angry man from the restaurant, Walter. He was red-faced and rumpled, clapping the men on the back and trying to hug the women. "Hey, I didn't know there was a party! Why wasn't I invited?" His voice boomed with false merriment. He picked up an empty bottle of champagne and brought it to his lips, confused when it was dry.

Emma knew she had to diffuse the awkward situation immediately. She walked right up to Walter and put her hand out to shake his. "Welcome, Walter. It's just a gathering of some of our family members and friends, but how nice it is for you to stop by. We're just about to have coffee and dessert. Follow me to the kitchen."

Distracted by her non-stop chatter, Walter let Emma take him by the arm. He sat where she indicated. She set a mug of black coffee and a plate of cookies down and sat across the table from him. Roger and Rob stood in the doorway, a solid presence, letting Emma know they would brook no further lousy behavior from Walter. She could see George hovering as well. Emma felt Walter would not calm down with three men glaring at him, so she asked George to take the coffee and tea carafes and dessert out to the main area so everyone could help themselves. Her discreet nod to George indicated she was all right.

Emma leaned across the table to Walter to engage him in the subjects she'd heard interested him, such as the Revolutionary and Civil Wars and his dairy farm. "I understand you had several ancestors who fought in the Revolutionary War. I did as well. I discovered that they are buried in the graveyard at the Old First Church in Bennington. How about yours? And I understand you run a wonderful dairy farm. I'd love to see it someday."

Walter began sobering up as he tried to focus on Emma's running commentary. "Yeah, the farm is a few miles past the covered bridge. It's small, but we do well." He held his cup up, taking in the café. "Um, could I get some more coffee?"

"Of course." Emma took a good look at Walter's face as she poured. His eyes were sad and tired-looking. His shoulders were slumped forward, almost in submission. But Emma was also aware that his anger could flare quickly. She trod softly but firmly. "I'd like to show you the store when you're done. I bet you'd be interested in some of the history books I ordered."

In the meantime, Rand quietly left the small group of partiers. He did not want to create a problem if Walter became conscious of his presence. When Emma felt Walter had settled down sufficiently, she looped her arm through his and led him out to the shelves of books. "Walking it off," she mouthed to the guests. He needed a distraction from the eyes of his fellow townspeople.

Emma brought Walter to the section on local history, talking about a book a friend of her father's had written about historic mementos he collected. "Charlie lived in Sunderland, and in his attic, he had a small museum with glass cases containing artillery from the Revolutionary and Civil Wars. He also had guns used by notorious criminals. There was a gun that John Dillinger had used in a bank robbery."

Walter was taking an interest in the books Emma was pointing out.

As the gathering started breaking up, Roger and Rob helped Walter with his jacket and walked him to the door, insisting they drive him home. It seemed all the bellicosity had left him, and he was somewhat agreeable.

Just as he reached the door's threshold, Walter suddenly turned back to search for Emma and acknowledged her graciousness with an embarrassed smile. "Thank you, Emma. I'll be back to buy some books." With a nod of goodbye, he let Rob drive him home, Roger following in Walter's truck.

After they left, Emma breathed a sigh of relief. June put an arm around her shoulders. "You did the absolute right thing, settling him down like that. I think you may have made a friend."

"I'm a little unsure whether that's a good thing," Emma confessed. "I think his mood can turn on a dime. I was lucky he was tired enough that I could distract him." Emma hoped that Walter would feel calmer after his visit and remain sober for the rest of the evening. She insisted she was all right and thanked everyone for coming. Her family stayed to help clean up. Always the worrier, Maggie decided to drive home with her mother and quiz her on who this drunk man was.

Once home, Emma begged off a cup of tea and went to bed, exhausted from dealing with Walter. Her family sat in the living room watching television and chatting about the afternoon's party. Emma looked out the window at the bright moon shining through the curtains and, as always, prayed for the well-being of everyone she loved and, now, for her new home and business as well. Tomorrow she would place the "Open for Business" sign on the old, wooden, front door of Moose on the Roof Books.

chapter fourteen
. . .

THE BOOKSTORE'S GRAND OPENING was, in fact, grand. Emma was overjoyed when so many acquaintances from Mill River and several tourists stopped in when they saw the unique new sign and the welcome mat in front of the door of the old church. The aroma of coffee and freshly baked scones filled the air as people browsed through the shelves.

Throughout the day, small groups of customers enjoyed relaxing in the café, sipping coffee or tea and munching on the cranberry scones Maggie baked in the café's oven. Emma was still unsure if Janie would agree to sell her baked goods for the bookstore. Maggie and Jack gave Emma an early Christmas gift, a wooden folk art carving of a moose with a matching rectangular piece hung below, etched with "The Moose Café." It looked perfect above the entrance.

During the weeks leading up to Christmas, Emma was pleased that her sales were more than adequate for a small-town bookstore. She was already thinking of ways to bring people into the store in the slump after the holidays. True to his word, a sober and subdued Walter made a few appearances at the shop. Other neighbors and new friends seemed happy to support a new business in town. Emma became accustomed to the types of books her patrons bought and ordered more mysteries, books about American history, and tomes written by current and former political pundits.

Christmas in Vermont brings to mind a Currier and Ives print of clean, sparkling snow frosting the mountains and fields and dusting the evergreen trees, black and white dairy cows and red barns dotting the countryside, and cross-country skiers and snowshoers plying the trails. Emma and George decided to treat their family to Christmas dinner at the Mill River Inn, a special indulgence after a busy few months. June sent a complimentary bottle of wine to the table, and the Nielsen family enjoyed the wonderful food and toasted each other's happiness and success. After they returned home, they sat in front of the fire, eating Emma's special apple crumb pie and exchanging gifts.

Emma closed the store the day after Christmas, and the family drove to Hildene, the summer home of President Lincoln's son, Robert Todd. Emma, Maggie, and Jack brought their cross-country skis to enjoy the beautiful trails around the property. George and Jennifer chose to tour the historic home, handsomely decorated for Christmas and warmed by a crackling fire in the living room. Wandering through the rooms, they listened to Christmas carols played on the lobby's antique player organ.

Jennifer and George, both history buffs, spent time taking in the displays of life at Hildene. President Lincoln's stovepipe hat, a vast bed said to have been constructed for a rotund President Taft for the nights he spent there, and the rooms occupied by Hildene's last resident, Lincoln's great-granddaughter, Peggy Beckwith. Peggy was a unique person who earned her pilot's license, began farming at the property, and allowed raccoons the run of the house according to local lore.

The next couple of months seemed to fly by. In January, Emma started a book club, which would meet in the café one Wednesday evening a month. They chose one of the books written by a local, well-known author. Emma and the librarians co-hosted a book and pajama night for kids in February. They served hot chocolate and popcorn, and the librarians took turns reading books to the children and their parents.

The Moose Café was becoming popular with locals and out-of-towners alike. The coffee and baked goods were top-notch. With some hesitation, Janie agreed to provide muffins and other bakery products twice a week. Emma would bake the remaining days.

One afternoon in February, Grace visited the bookstore. Emma sensed that the woman was shy, so she just said a quick hello and let her browse. After a while, Emma approached Grace and asked if she could help select a book. Grace seemed unsure.

"Let me buy you a cup of coffee, and we can sit down and figure out what interests you," Emma said. The two women settled themselves at the pine table in the café, and Emma poured two cups of coffee and put out a couple of apple cinnamon muffins. "On the house, Grace. I'm glad to have someone to visit. It's been a slow day."

Emma and Grace talked about books, and the conversation meandered to how they both came to live in Mill River. Grace explained that she grew up on a dairy farm cooperative not far away. "My parents were kind of like hippies. When I was old enough to fend for myself, they moved to Oregon. Walter came to the farm once to see the operation. He was so mature and self-assured, and that attracted me. We started dating, and within a year, we were married." Walter used more modern techniques, and the farm became quite successful. Grace took to farm life like a duck to water. She had helped on the cooperative farm with the hens and goats, gathered eggs, made bread, and had begun learning the rudiments of making cheese. She knew how to coax milk out of a reluctant cow, and her domestic skills were much appreciated by her new husband.

Emma was charmed by Grace's story and realized she quite liked the woman sitting across from her. As Grace took another sip from her coffee mug, Emma noticed a small bruise circling Grace's wrist, poking out from her sweater. Grace lowered her eyes and pulled the sleeve down. "You know, Emma, Walter speaks very highly of you," Grace said, trying to divert Emma's attention.

"I'm sorry he was difficult at your party."

"Oh, past history," Emma said. "He calmed down rather quickly. I think I talked him to death." Emma asked Grace about her children, not wanting the conversation to become awkward.

Grace's face lit up as she talked about them. "We have three. Jesse's the oldest, fourteen, and he's in ninth grade. The twins are ten, Ellie and Lizabeth. They're in fifth and such smart girls. Jesse likes working with his hands better. I think he would be happy to take over the farm someday."

"It sounds like you are so proud of them. And it's so nice to think about continuing a family farm. So many small farms are folding these days."

"I know, but if we can branch out beyond selling milk to stores and creameries, we could really do well. I'd love to get some goats and start making artisanal cheese." Grace's eyes shone with anticipation as she talked about her ideas.

"Does Walter feel that way, too?"

Grace hesitated. "I'm really not sure. Right now, he's concentrating on making sure our dairy clients are happy and trying to find a few more buyers. He works on the farm, does the books, and travels to meet with potential clients. I think he's too busy to think about adding to the operation." Grace lowered her eyes and moved her hands onto her lap, unconsciously pulling down her sleeves. She hesitated before she spoke but then confessed that evenings could be difficult. "I make sure his dinner is ready and try to keep the kids out of his hair, but..." It was then that Emma noticed a tear running down Grace's cheek. The younger woman turned away, embarrassed, silently wiping away even more tears. She was not used to someone so caring and listening without judgment.

"Grace, it's all right. You don't owe me any explanation, but I'm here to listen if that's what you need."

Grace took a deep breath, wondering if she could trust this woman with the kind eyes seated across the table. There weren't many people in whom she could confide. Surprising even herself, the words came gushing out. "I know I shouldn't talk about my husband. I'm sure you've heard stories about him, and you saw for yourself what he's like when he drinks.

My best friend, Janie, keeps telling me I should leave him, that he'll hurt me or one of the kids someday, that he has a mean streak that he can't control. But where would I go? I can't leave my kids, and if I took them, he would come after us."

Grace took a minute to compose herself, and Emma refreshed her coffee mug. "Janie just doesn't understand. Her husband, Mike, is a great guy, so gentle and patient. I just wish..." Grace suddenly leaned across the table, an intense expression in her eyes. "Emma, have you ever wondered if you could go back in time and end up with a different life?" And in the next second, she backtracked. "Don't listen to me! I'm not making any sense. I would never want a life without Jesse and the twins." Looking at her watch, Grace became nervous. "I need to hurry home now. I've been away much longer than I said I would be."

"Grace, wait, you came into the bookstore to find a book. I know just the thing." Emma walked over to the cooking section and quickly selected a book on cheesemaking. "Here you go. My gift to you. I'll be your first customer when you make your goat cheese."

"That's so nice of you. Thank you! And thank you for listening to me. You won't say anything to Walter, will you?"

Emma took Grace's hands into her own. "Of course not. Enjoy the book, and I hope to see you soon." Emma poured another cup of coffee and wondered just what it was about her life that Grace would have changed. Emma remembered June explaining how close Grace and Rand had become. Was Grace thinking of him? A few customers were milling about, and Emma had to pull her musings back from Grace's dilemma.

Emma spent the rest of the afternoon helping customers, making sure the café was well stocked, and processing book orders. She remained disturbed, though, by that bracelet of a bruise around Grace's wrist.

March brought both mud and maple syrup season to Vermont. As Emma drove to the bookstore in the mornings, she smiled to see smoke rising from several smokehouses along the way. She considered asking one of the owners if she could feature bottles of their syrup in the bookstore. And in a bow to the ever-present mud, Emma placed a boot scraper at the store's front door.

One blustery, cloudy morning, the door to the bookstore swung open, letting in a burst of cold air. Emma's eyes widened as she took in the woman framed in the doorway. She resembled a portrait by Modigliani. She had long brunette curls surrounding a perfect oval face, a graceful neck, and she wore a composed, confident look in her eyes. Scanning the bookstore, the woman set her eyes on Emma and stepped forward.

chapter fifteen
. . .

"I BELIEVE YOU ARE Emma Nielsen," she said as she strode across the floor toward Emma. "My name is Cassandra Adams." Emma shook Cassandra's outstretched hand, noticing that her grip was firm, but her smile softened her strong features.

"How can I help you? Are you looking for a particular book?"

"No, I came to talk to you about a thought I had. Maybe we can help each other. Do you have a few minutes?"

"Of course," said Emma, glancing around the room. She told the couple of customers browsing through the shelves that she would be in the café if they needed her. "Why don't you come into the café for a cup of coffee…or tea? We have either."

"A cup of tea would be nice, please. This is just lovely," Cassandra murmured as she took in the quaint café.

After Emma had served the drinks and set out a plate of cookies, she folded her arms in front of her and looked at Cassandra inquisitively.

"Emma, I am a psychologist and author, and I've just written a book about society's responses to death, dying, and bereavement. I would love it if you included my book in your store, but I also spend time talking about the subject to groups. Have you ever heard of Death Café?"

"Yes, I have, and I've actually always wanted to attend one."

"Wonderful!" exclaimed Cassandra. "Would you be interested in having something like that in the bookstore? We can't call it a Death Café, but maybe 'Talking About Death'? The name of my book is 'Last Thoughts'."

"I have heard of several bookstores and libraries featuring Death Café Nights. Would your program be similar?"

"I thought I could make copies of individual chapters of my book, have them available to anyone interested, and then discuss them on the night we meet. But wherever the discussion leads would be fine with me. If you're interested, I will give you my credentials and names of colleagues you can call for references."

Emma indicated that she was intrigued after having dealt with death during her work in a nursing home, as well as with friends and family members. "Cassandra, I think this might be a terrific idea, but I am relatively new in town and would like to scope out the level of interest before committing. Let me talk to a few people I know, and I'll call you probably next week. Does that work?"

Cassandra agreed. She left her personal and professional information with Emma and clasped Emma's hands in hers. She smiled charmingly and was gone, swooping through the door as dramatically as she entered.

"Wait till I tell George. Half the men in town will be signing up to talk about death to gawk at her," thought Emma.

That evening, as Emma and George drank their cups of tea after dinner, she shared Cassandra's visit to the bookstore, her idea for the program, and that she found Cassandra charismatic, intelligent, and beautiful. "She may be a huge draw, George. And I think what she has to say would be fascinating and thought-provoking. She gave me a copy of her book."

"It will be April by the time Cassandra starts her meetings. Is spring the right time to be talking about something so grim?"

"That's a good thought," responded Emma. "But it will be lighter out in the evening, and that means people will be more willing to leave their houses to attend it. I'm going to talk to June and Caleb and get their thoughts. Maybe the women I know at the library." Emma put her cup on the coffee table and turned to her husband. "George, tell me the truth. If it were not our bookstore offering it, would you go to a discussion on death?"

"If I'm being honest, I don't think so. Living with Parkinson's makes me feel more vulnerable these days. And I've never been good at sharing my feelings, especially with people I don't know well."

Emma hugged her husband. "I do understand. I've spent so much of my career counseling patients and their grieving families that it's more comfortable for me. But I will admit that the older I get when I think of my own mortality, it is a bit more unnerving."

Over the next week, Emma talked to several people whose opinions she respected. She was heartened to discover that they were all open to at least attending one "death" meeting. So, Emma called Cassandra, and they made plans to hold the discussion group in several weeks. Emma felt that for the first meeting, she would initially invite people she knew to act as a test case. The table in the café held twelve people, so the meeting would be limited to that number. Cassandra said she would email Emma an outline of what she would cover and the questions she would ask to initiate a discussion.

Easter arrived, and daffodils and grape hyacinths grew wild along the roadways, with wisteria vines hugging split rail fences. Spring-green grass poked through the soil, and there was new growth on trees. After a long winter, the air smelled sweet and fresh. George began working the soil in the backyard garden at the cottage, insisting that the exercise kept his legs limber. Emma enlisted eight people to attend Cassandra's program. Emma, George, and Cassandra would make eleven, and Emma asked Janie if she would provide the coffee cake for the evening. Janie agreed and offered to bring it herself.

Emma began feeling apprehensive as the appointed evening arrived. She had held several programs at the bookstore, but this one was sure to be emotional and perhaps controversial. Emma and George arrived early and started brewing coffee and hot water for tea, then set out plates and mugs. Emma lit a fragrant orange spice candle. Cassandra arrived, and Emma introduced her to George. Glancing at George for a reaction, she wasn't surprised when her poker-faced husband barely twitched an eyelid. Cassandra was outfitted elegantly in a calf-length navy blue dress with a Pashmina scarf draped around her shoulders. Her dark hair formed loose waves around her pretty face.

The attendees began ambling into the café, greeting one another and chatting animatedly. Emma introduced Cassandra to June, Roger, Caleb and Rebecca, and librarians Caroline and Marie. Last to arrive were Grace and Walter. Emma detected some surprise and guarded looks when Walter took a seat, but she hoped the evening's discussion would dissipate any unease. When everyone was seated, Emma asked Cassandra to talk about her work and the book she wrote.

Cassandra explained her belief that given the opportunity, many people wanted to share their experiences with the death of family and friends. "What I think we should start with is one of the chapters of my book that asks how we live our lives knowing there is death. How do we not become depressed? How do we find joy every day? I'd like to open that up for your ideas."

Emma thought Father Hill would be the first to respond, and he proved her right. "I think you have to choose every day to find your purpose, whatever makes you fulfilled and happy. It helps to feel needed by other people."

His wife nodded her head. "Giving of yourself takes the attention away from yourself and whatever is troubling you. So many people suffer from anxiety, not only anxiety about death."

Grace was wide-eyed with interest in this unique discussion. "I probably love animals more than people, well, except for my family," she said, blushing. "They are God's creatures, too, and I cry when one of them dies. I love spending my day with them, feeding, milking, birthing. They bring me so much joy."

Cassandra agreed this was a good point. Suddenly, it seemed everyone wanted to say something, and Emma was relieved that the attendees were comfortable with the topic. Janie had arrived and was setting out the coffee cake.

Emma and George poured coffee and tea just as Rand popped his head around the doorway. "Oh, hey, Emma. I just came in looking for a book. I didn't realize you had something going on."

Emma explained they were trying a pilot program, and if he were interested, he would be welcome to take the last seat at the table. He suddenly noticed Grace and Walter. He took his seat hesitantly and tried to avoid Walter's glare.

Somewhat distracted by the tension she felt emanating from Walter, Emma poured Marie's hot water over a tea bag the librarian had pulled from her purse. Marie explained that she brought the herbal tea since she could not tolerate caffeine in the evening. Janie put down a piece of coffee cake in front of Marie and, curious about the discussion, hopped onto the countertop to listen to the rest of the program.

As the group drank and complimented Janie on her delicious cake, they settled into a comfortable discussion, with Cassandra adding her thoughts to facilitate the conversation. As Roger was talking about coping with becoming a widower the previous year, Caroline became aware that Marie was in distress. Marie was clutching her throat, having difficulty breathing. There was fear and confusion in her eyes. Roger was quickly at her side, trying to calm her down and asking for a window to be opened and for a cold compress. Rand just as quickly dialed emergency services on his cell phone.

"Tell them to hurry, Rand," Roger said. She's having trouble breathing, and her pulse is racing."

With worry knitting her brow, Caroline kneeled beside her friend and held her hand as they waited. George, as a former police officer, was accustomed to directing people during emergencies. He asked the remainder of the group to go out into the main part of the bookstore to give Marie air and space for paramedics to work when they arrived. Emma retrieved a cool washcloth to place on Marie's forehead.

Father Cal took charge once Rebecca, Cassandra, Walter, Grace, and Janie left the café. He spoke calmly. "Let's have a word of prayer for Marie," and he asked the group to form a circle and hold hands. Walter looked dubious, but Grace pleaded with her eyes for him to cooperate. Janie took surreptitious glances back at the café. She was anxious to know what was happening.

Paramedics and police arrived quickly and filled the small room with life-saving equipment, rapidly administering oxygen and asking Roger to describe what happened.

That evening, one person in the bookstore was paying close attention to the events unfolding in the small café where Marie had fallen ill. Dark thoughts and ill intentions were coalescing, much like a darkening sky and low-hanging clouds of a storm over the mountains surrounding Mill River.

chapter sixteen
• • •

THE AMBULANCE SPED AWAY from the bookstore toward the hospital in Bennington, followed by Rand and Caroline in Rand's truck. The small group, gathered once again in the café, were upset about what they had just witnessed. Emma told everyone she would call them when she heard how Marie was. Janie surprised Emma by offering to stay and help clean up, but Emma thanked her and sent her back to her restaurant. "I'm sure your husband can always use an extra pair of hands in the kitchen. But thank you so much for baking the coffee cake. It was excellent, as always." Emma felt the icy relationship between herself and Janie was beginning to thaw. Nevertheless, Emma always felt she had to be overly solicitous to the moody younger woman.

Roger seemed lost in thought. "I hope she's okay. One minute, she was fine, and the next...you never know. Life is so fragile, isn't it?"

Walter, arms crossed in front of his broad chest, just shook his head and looked at Cassandra with a nasty glint in his eyes.

"Well, well, well. Cassandra Adams, you sure you're not related to Morticia?"

Grace looked at him in horror.

"Hey, don't blame me," he said, shaking his hands in mock horror. "Here we are talking about dying and what happens. One of us keels over!"

Cassandra straightened her shoulders and approached the farmer. "We do not know what happened yet. And I will chalk that remark up to your discomfort. We don't always know how to react when faced with a sudden crisis or death."

"Hey, if you can't take a joke..." Walter's laughter died when he realized no one appreciated his humor, and his face reddened with anger and resentment.

George diplomatically tried to diffuse the tension in the room. He gently steered Walter toward the door, letting him know they would call him and Grace with any information. Emma winced when she saw Walter's grip on his wife's arm as they left. He was not accustomed to having a woman stand up to him, and he was angry and embarrassed.

George once again took charge by putting the kettle on and making tea. "Ladies, please sit and relax. Cassandra, would you like to wait with us to find out how Marie is? It may be a while."

"Yes, thank you, George."

"I'm anxious to know as well," added Emma, concern creasing her brow. And I feel responsible since whatever it was, it happened here."

Hoping to deflect those thoughts, George directed his attention to their guest. "Cassandra. That's a beautiful name. What's the origin?"

"It's Greek, as am I. My mother loved mythology. She is an actress in Athens, still a beautiful woman in her seventies, and very dramatic. Growing up, I was always Cass-ahn-dra, with a flourish." Cassandra swept her Pashmina-draped arm theatrically.

Emma sipped her tea and sent a silent look of gratitude to her husband for being so thoughtful in making Cassandra feel welcome and comfortable. She asked Cassandra about her father.

"He is retired from a civil service job in Athens. They love city life but have a beach house where they go to relax. He is also artistic. He paints in watercolor. I have a couple of his seascapes in our house in Bennington."

George wanted to know how she came to live in Vermont. "I met my husband while he was on vacation in Greece, visiting one of my family's acquaintances. After we were introduced, we saw each other almost daily and decided to keep in touch when he returned to the States. Eventually, I followed him to Vermont since I could practice and write anywhere. We were married at Hildene, at that beautiful stone wall overlooking the countryside. James is a professor of math at Bennington College."

"You will have to meet June's husband, Rob," said Emma. "He taught psychology at Bennington. You two may have a lot in common. He was not here tonight since he had to oversee an event at the Inn." Emma got up to pour more hot water over her tea bag.

Finally, her cell phone rang, and she quickly answered. "Rand! Please tell me Marie will be all right."

"She will be," Rand assured her. "Marie is recovering from a severe anaphylactic attack. The doctor theorizes that her tea may have contained some foreign substance. The lab will figure it out. Marie says she bought the tea online from a third-party seller, probably a fly-by-night deal. Geez, I've seen clients come in with their dogs or cats sick after feeding them some supposedly organic stuff they've bought online."

"We appreciate your staying with Marie. Please tell her we are praying for her." Emma hung up the phone and told George and Cassandra how Marie had become sick. All three breathed a sigh of relief that the librarian would be okay.

Cassandra got up to rinse her mug in the sink and walked to the coat rack to get her things. "Emma, we don't have to talk about this right now, but I would understand if you did not want to continue with my program. What Walter said may be just what other people are thinking."

"Oh, please. What Walter said was just rude and insensitive. I think everyone enjoyed our time together tonight and would want it to continue."

They walked to the front door together and stepped outside into the chilly evening. Cassandra, whom Emma still found a little intimidating, unexpectedly pulled Emma into a hug. "I know tonight was difficult for you, and I thank you for your kindness to me. But Emma, even aside from Walter, I sensed an undercurrent of tension here tonight. Emma and George, you must be careful."

They stood, framed in the front door, as they waved goodbye. They stepped outside to gaze at the full moon, and George turned to his wife. "So, do you think our Cassandra is a bit of a prophetess?" he asked with raised eyebrows. "I saw the looks Roger and Rand were giving Walter." George put his arm around Emma's shoulders. "I don't mind telling you tonight made me a little nervous." He absentmindedly chewed his bottom lip as he looked out into the night. Emma saw the concern on her husband's face. She leaned against his solid frame. "Don't you worry. Marie will be fine. And, so will we." While Emma, Cassandra, and George had been drinking tea and talking about their lives, they were unaware of the commotion a short way down the road. After leaving the bookstore, Roger, Janie, Walter, and Grace headed to their cars.

Roger, however, made the mistake of confronting Walter and rebuking him for his remark about Cassandra's name. "So clever, aren't you, Walter? Making that rude comment to her not a moment after the ambulance left with Marie. You have no respect for anyone, and you're a bully to boot. Always have been." Roger became more animated with each word.

Shrugging off Grace, who was trying in vain to pull him away, Walter stood nose to nose with Roger, his face red and scowling. "Last time I heard, it was a free country, and I can say whatever I please. You're still pissed at me 'cause you've never gotten over what happened to your precious daughter."

"My daughter chose the wrong people to hang out with that day, but you didn't have to make her life miserable in school." Roger tried to rein in his anger, but thoughts of Lauren's humiliation at school weren't helping.

"Can't help it if she was ugly to begin with," Walter spat out.

Grace had had enough and insisted that Walter stop talking and get in the car. Walter swerved around to face her. "I will leave when I decide to leave!" With that, he grabbed Grace's arm tightly, dragging her along to the truck and slamming the passenger door after she got in. He got behind the wheel and gunned the engine, leaving a trail of smoke and venom in his wake.

Eyes wide, Janie turned around to Roger. "What was all that about?" Janie realized that Roger's breathing was ragged. He was bent at the waist, hands resting on his knees. "Roger, are you all right?"

Roger stood up and waved away her concern. "Damn it, I'm sorry you had to see that. I cannot abide that man."

"But what was that about your daughter?" Janie was younger and had not grown up in Mill River. She did not know the history between Roger and Walter.

Roger, shoulders hunched forward and hands shoved into the pockets of his barn jacket, found that he didn't have the energy or desire to tell Janie what had happened. "He ruined her life, Janie," he replied almost in a whisper. "I'll leave it at that."

Unsure of how to respond, Janie told Roger how sorry she was. "That man has no heart. I worry about Grace, and her kids, of course."

"You know, most of the time, Walter can put a good face on in public. But you saw how he grabbed Grace and pushed her into the truck. I can't imagine what it's like for the kids in that household. They see and understand more than we think they do, for sure."

"So, what's the solution?" Janie wondered.

Roger stared in the direction Walter's truck had gone. "Not sure I even care to say." He turned toward his car and headed home.

Janie stood there for a while, looking at the car's taillights. She thought about Roger's cryptic reply and how frightened

Grace looked as Walter dragged her to the truck. Janie understood abuse. Abusers rarely change. She certainly didn't think Walter was capable of it.

Janie glanced back at the bookstore. Through the stained-glass windows, she could see the shadows of Emma, George, and Cassandra. Though the night was cloudy and starless, the moon poked through wispy clouds and cast an eerie light on the graves in the back of the store. There was a chill in the air, and Janie shivered through her light jacket. It was April, usually a time of hope and renewal.

As Janie walked to her truck, however, her thoughts were anything but hopeful. If she had noticed the look of longing that passed between Rand and Grace, Walter must have as well. What had Walter done to Roger's daughter? Janie opened the door to her pick-up and got behind the steering wheel. She sat quietly, thinking about Marie, Emma, her new bookstore, and café. Finally, Janie turned the key in the ignition and drove home to Mike...and to the life she desperately needed.

chapter seventeen
. . .

MARIE SPENT THE NIGHT in the hospital under observation, and Caroline brought her friend home the following morning. Marie was in her mid-fifties and had never married, so she appreciated the support of friends and co-workers. In turn, her loyal cadre of friends appreciated Marie's cheerfulness and the homemade goodies she baked as thank-you gifts.

While George minded the bookshop on Saturday, Emma brought the librarian a bouquet of flowers, chicken noodle soup, and biscuits from the Mill River Inn. Marie still looked pale but insisted on putting the kettle on for tea (regular black tea!) and placing a cookie plate on the kitchen table. "I have to apologize. I've had these cookies in the freezer. Just took them out this morning to give Caroline a few."

"They look delicious, Marie." Emma sat at an antique maple table and looked around the French country kitchen. "I love the way you've decorated. So, tell me, how are you feeling?"

"So much better. I can't tell you how grateful I am for drinking that tea with people who knew what they were doing:

a nurse, a pharmacist, and a veterinarian. I was in excellent hands. From now on, I will always carry my Epi-pen with me."

Emma took a nibble of a superb chocolate chip cookie. "What are you allergic to," asked Emma.

"That's just it. I was diagnosed long ago with something called idiopathic anaphylaxis. It means that it's unclear what sets off my reaction. I haven't had any allergy problems in years. There had to be something in that tea. The lab is investigating." Marie shook her head in annoyance at her naivety. "I'll never order from an unregulated seller again."

Emma told Marie what happened after the ambulance whisked her away. "Cassandra wondered if we would want her to continue her program. I assured her that everyone seemed to enjoy the evening. Walter also had a snarky comment comparing her to Morticia Addams."

"Well, that sounds like something Walter would say. I can't figure out that man."

"Join the club. We've had some nice conversations about his farm and his interest in local history. But there's another side to him, isn't there?" Emma finished her cookie and tea. "I have to get going, Marie. I'm so glad you are all right. When you're up to it, why don't we discuss a couple more joint programs we can hold at the bookstore? I also wanted to let you know that I've bought some nice herbal tea for the café. It's from the supermarket, a brand we all know."

Marie laughed as she walked Emma to the door. "Thank you so much for stopping by. I'll enjoy the soup and biscuits for lunch."

Emma left Marie's little cottage, which stood picturesquely on a hill a block from the library. From there, she thought how beautiful the mountains looked and smiled when she saw shoots of crocus and early daffodils in the front garden.

Saturday was also the day the farmer's market was held at the Grange Hall. As she often did, Grace visited Janie that morning, bringing two cups of coffee with her. Janie set out two Morning Glory muffins, and Grace sat behind the table displaying jams, herbs, and baked goods for sale. Janie looked closely at her friend, alarmed at the dark circles under her eyes.

Reading Janie's expression, Grace sighed. "I know I look like death warmed over. I didn't sleep well last night. So, go ahead and say what's on your mind, but I can't be too long. Walter's expecting me back in an hour."

"What is he, your keeper? Honey, that man has too much control over you. Did he hurt you last night?"

"Oh, he just ranted about how I needed to keep my mouth shut when he had something to say. I just felt awful at how he treated Cassandra."

"After Walter took off, Roger said Walter ruined his daughter's life. Do you know anything about it?"

"I once mentioned that poor girl's face to him, but I sure got the message never to ask him again. It happened a long time ago."

"Look, sweetie, you know Mike's mother has that big old house, and there's more than enough room for you and the kids. All you have to do is walk out the door."

"You're a good friend to worry about me." Grace's long bangs hid the tears forming in the corner of her eyes. "If I leave, you know he won't leave me alone. He'll never let the kids go. If I walked out, he would say I abandoned them.

I need to stay with them." After a beat, Grace looked purposefully at Janie. "It's awful to say, but I almost wish he would get angry enough to have a heart attack or a stroke or something. But he takes medicine that supposedly keeps his heart... What was it the doctor said? In rhythm, that's it. And there's something that thins his blood so he doesn't have a stroke."

"It's not awful at all." When medicine was mentioned, however, Janie was suddenly alert. "Do you know the names?"

"What, the medications? I don't remember, but I'm the one who picks them up from the pharmacy. You know Walter doesn't want to have to deal with Roger."

Their conversation was interrupted several times by customers buying Janie's homemade jams and muffins and asking about the uses of the herbs she foraged and dried. When the last customer left, Janie seemed lost in thought.

"Hey, you look like your mind is miles away," teased Grace.

"Medications," whispered Janie. Her tone was ominous. Turning to Grace, she said, "Find out what they are. You know," she shrugged casually. "...food for thought."

chapter eighteen
...

GRACE STARED AT HER friend in shock. "Are you suggesting what I think you are? Oh, Janie, I may wish for something, but to act on it? Never!"

"All right, all right," Janie held her hands up in supplication. "But, please, Grace, promise you'll come to us if you feel in danger. I don't trust that man, and you need to keep your eyes open."

"I do promise," Grace said. "I have to get back to the farm. Thanks for the muffin, and I'll take a jar of blueberry jam. I'll pay you later, okay? See you soon!" She hopped off the stool and hugged Janie goodbye.

Janie watched her friend weave through the stalls, greeting other farm families and bending down to say hi to their young children and dogs. "Such a kind-hearted person," Janie thought. She noticed how thin and vulnerable Grace looked. With her long, strawberry-blonde hair pulled into a messy ponytail, she looked like a teenager. Janie knew Grace would never be a match for Walter's bullying.

Janie's thoughts were suddenly pulled back by customers

milling about at her food display. The sales were good this morning, and Janie looked forward to returning to the restaurant and giving her husband a hand with dinner preparation. She knew she was one of the lucky ones. Mike and his mother, Ronnie, had embraced her and given her a warm, family home. Hopefully, one day soon, when money wasn't tight, they would welcome a child into their family. As far as Janie was concerned, she was living a charmed life, one she never thought she would have...or deserve.

Emma and George attended the early evening service at the church across from the bookstore. They enjoyed Father Cal's sermons, and his sense of humor always shone through the more serious aspects of religious faith. The service was casual, featuring a small band and a choir leading the congregation in more current praise songs. After the service, Cal and Rebecca were invited to the Nielsens' cottage for dinner.

When Cal and Rebecca arrived, George showed them into the cozy dining room. Up to the chair rail, the wall was covered in knotty pine panels; the upper half of the wall was a creamy white with hand-stenciled vines circling the room just under the ceiling. The punched tin chandelier overhead cast a soft light over the dinner table. Emma had prepared chili, honey cornbread, and a fruit bowl in the morning and simply had to serve from the crockpot for a quick dinner. After dinner and conversation about the sermon, the foursome moved into the living room for coffee and dessert. George played soft music and lit a fire in the fireplace since the Vermont evenings were still cool.

Cal was entranced by Annie, who jumped onto his lap and settled in, purring loudly. "I guess she knows I'm an animal lover," said Cal as he stroked the cat's soft fur. "My family had barn cats all the time. They worked hard for their keep!"

"I can't imagine Annie actually catching any critter," George said. "If she sees a bug, she just pats it with her big, soft paws and stares at it. Maybe she thinks she's guarding it." He laughed fondly at the gentle cat's antics.

Emma brought in a plate of shortbread cookies and poured coffee for everyone. The conversation shifted to Marie and the fate of Cassandra's program.

Rebecca reached for a cookie. "We visited Marie a couple of days after her discharge and are so relieved that she will be just fine. Hopefully, Cassandra will want to continue sharing her book."

"I believe she will. We know that Marie's episode was an accident. She should have been carrying an Epi-pen," Emma quickly added.

"So, Emma, I want to know how those crows are treating you," said Cal, a mischievous smile on his lips. "Any more Hitchcockian moments?"

Laughing, Emma explained that she did enjoy seeing them. "I leave them some bits of leftover muffins and cake. They always seem to be watching from the steeple and swoop down immediately to get the goodies. I meant to mention that they are leaving little trinkets on the window sill of the steeple and the stone pillar at the entrance to the graveyard. Bottle caps, pieces of twine, things like that. Do you think they're leaving me gifts?"

"Seems so. I think doing that reinforces your putting out treats. I told you they're smart!"

"They remind me of those scary birds in Hitchcock's movie," interjected George, the former cop. "I'm not really a fan of that genre. Emma's crazy about mysteries. I'm more of a Godfather/Law and Order kind of guy."

"Ever since we moved here and our workload has decreased, we've been bingeing old comedy shows. We're in the middle of re-watching The Office. The silliness offsets some of the seriousness of my job," offered Cal.

Emma asked the couple how they came to live and work in Mill River.

"Cal went to college with Roger McGarrity," Rebecca said. "They both had work/study jobs in the administrative offices and became friends. They stayed in touch over the years, and when Roger let us know that a position was available for a pastor here, we knew we were ready for a change. A small-town church is just right for us. Emma, tell us how you and George decided to move to Vermont and start your new enterprise."

"You could say we were also ready for a change. We have always loved this part of Vermont, and, well, it was my dream to open a bookstore. I thought the old Congregational church was the perfect place, and it was available at a reasonable price since it had been vacant for so long. Our kids thought we would just sit home, watch television, and do crosswords all day after we retired. They were shocked when we told them our plans."

"Our children never think their old parents can learn new tricks," Cal said. "I think the secret to a healthy and satisfying life is to continue to do something meaningful. Retirement shouldn't mean that you stop working or contributing in some way. I love being a minister, counseling, writing sermons, and participating in the community. It keeps my mind sharp."

Emma took a sip of her coffee. "Your friend, Roger, says he wants to retire and hopes his granddaughter takes over his business. He doesn't seem like the kind of man to sit back either."

"Not at all," replied Cal. "Roger has a new cabin up in the mountains where he can fish and hike to his heart's content. His granddaughter is a bright young woman and will be more than capable once she learns the business."

"Last time I was there picking up prescriptions..." Emma wondered. "There was a woman hunched over the computer behind the counter. She didn't look up when I talked to Roger, which I thought was unusual. Most people here are amiable and talkative."

"Ah, that's a sad story," sighed Cal, "That's Lauren, Roger's daughter. She does the ordering and billing. She prefers to stay behind the scenes."

Naturally curious about people, Emma wanted to know what it was about Lauren that was sad. George took the opportunity to refill everyone's mug and swipe another cookie from the plate on the coffee table.

Rebecca looked at her husband for confirmation before speaking. "I guess this isn't really gossip. It's well known that Lauren has had a difficult life. She was disfigured in a snow tubing accident in high school. She ripped her cheek open when the tube smashed into a metal wire poking out from a fence at the bottom of a steep icy hill. Even though she had surgery, the scar never healed properly. Some of the other students ridiculed her and called her horrible names. She lost her self-confidence, tried to go to college, but dropped out."

"Lauren went through a period of acting out," said Cal, taking up the story from there. "She wound up pregnant.

Roger and his wife, Marjorie, were very supportive of Lauren and encouraged her to have the baby. They helped raise the child, and Katie has grown up as a real blessing to Lauren and Roger. Unfortunately, Margie passed away last year." Cal explained that Lauren always kept a low profile around town because some of the students who humiliated her all those years ago still live and work here. "My buddy, Roger, has never come to terms with those kids. Well, they're grown-ups now."

"Would Walter Eammons be one of those people?" Emma asked. "I've seen Roger and Walter together, and there's definitely tension between them."

"Yes, he was one of them. He was what you might call the leader of that clique. One of the girls invited Lauren, who was shy and naïve, to go tubing and skiing with them that day. Walter and a few of his football buddies decided to make her life miserable. Can you imagine how she felt when they nicknamed her Frankenstein? At that age in high school, the acceptance of your peers is everything. Roger has tried to forgive Walter for his own peace of mind, but his heart hurts for Lauren, so he finds it impossible."

"Walter is...difficult," Emma thoughtfully replied. I can see that aspect of his personality." Emma leaned forward, hesitating before speaking. Cal, can I tell you something in confidence?"

"Of course. Do you want to talk to me privately?"

"No, that's not necessary. It's just that the last time Grace was in the bookstore, we had a cup of coffee and chatted for a while. She's such a sweet person. But I was alarmed to see a bruise encircling her wrist. It was evident that someone had held on to her tightly. I'm pretty sure that someone was Walter."

The minister was silent for a moment and folded his hands under his chin as if in prayer. "Yes, I've wondered about them. You know, someone in my line of work hears a lot of talk in a town this small. Grace and Walter are not often in church, but I will keep an eye out for Grace and try to let her know my door is always open."

"Thanks, Cal. I know you will."

"And now, I think Rebecca and I had better get back to our fur babies before they tear the house apart looking for kibble."

"Thank you so much for a delicious dinner," Rebecca said. It's been nice spending the evening with you."

Emma and George walked the minister and his wife to the front door and waved as their car backed out of the driveway and headed back into town. After shutting the front door, George turned around, his legs suddenly refusing to move. Emma noticed and realized her husband was experiencing episodes like this more often.

"Honey, you're supposed to see the neurologist later in May. What do you think about calling him on Monday and seeing if we can get an earlier appointment?" Dr Shah had made no changes in George's therapeutics at their last appointment, but Emma thought it might be time to talk about increasing the Parkinson's medication.

"Well, I could say no, but I know that look. You've been in social worker mode all night. Sure, go ahead and call." He gave his wife a stern look. "But for goodness sake, please remember that we're still newcomers. Let's slow down when it comes to getting involved in complex relationships. It sounds like the issues between Roger and Walter took root long ago. And Grace and Walter need professional counseling."

Lying in bed that night, Emma looked out her window at the dark sky. When she found sleep elusive, she thought about the people in her life whom she missed and her family and friends who were no longer alive. She thought, as well, about the people in her life now who seemed troubled. Of course, she knew George was right. But offering help to people who were hurting, even if it was just listening to them over a cup of coffee, was second nature to her. Before sleep overtook her, Emma thought of the intricate and complicated web she had discovered in her new home of Mill River.

chapter nineteen
. . .

EMMA AND GEORGE DROVE to Bennington for the rescheduled appointment with Dr Shah. The air was fresh and fragrant, and green sprigs of grass and early wildflowers shot up along the side of the road. As Emma drove, George closed his eyes and, feeling the sun's warmth, enjoyed the sensation of peace it brought. He had been anxious about the new symptom of his legs "freezing."

Emma looked over at her husband, sensing his concern about the appointment. "I have a feeling that everything will be fine. Dr Shah will know just what to do for you."

George was used to the quick physical and mental examinations the neurologist and his nurse gave. Dr Shah reiterated that hesitancy in initiating walking and occasional visual disturbances were quite common in Parkinson's patients. He decided to increase George's medication, a common one taken by many people with the neurological disorder. He did caution, however, that with a change in medication, George might experience more frequent hallucinations. There was a drug for that, too, but Dr Shah preferred a wait-and-see approach.

Since Moose on the Roof Books was closed on Mondays, Emma and George had lunch in the city at Riverside Deli, a delicatessen they had taken their children to often years ago. Riverside Deli had a fun, youthful vibe, terrific homemade soup, and overfilled sandwiches. "Oh, Gosh, I am full," George said as he patted his stomach. Maybe we should walk a bit. I'd like to check out that old stationery store. They have things you can't find on Amazon."

"Really? How is that possible," laughed Emma. "Let's drive over and park in front. We can window shop for a while. I also want to get more herbal tea, and I'd love to stop at Bennington Potters. I've got my eye on that pretty blue teapot."

After completing their errands, Emma and George returned to Mill River to pick up the prescription at Roger's pharmacy.

"Let me know how you're feeling on this new dosage," Roger advised as he handed the package to George. It may take some time to adjust."

As George and Roger talked, Emma noticed the woman at the computer. "Hi," Emma called, deciding to introduce herself. "I'm Emma Nielsen, and the man talking to Roger is my husband, George. Would you be Lauren?"

The woman swiveled slightly in her chair, her long brown hair falling over part of her face. She smiled shyly and nodded. "Yes, I'm Lauren. I hear your bookstore is wonderful. I wish you lots of luck." She quickly turned back to the computer.

Hoping to extend the conversation, Emma offered an invitation. "Well, please come in anytime and have a cup of coffee with me. We see your dad fairly often."

Lauren inadvertently tucked her hair behind her ear as she returned to work, and Emma froze as she saw the scar on

Lauren's cheek. A jagged and raised pink line ran from just below her eye to her chin. Her eye was pulled slightly down due to the puckering of the scar. Emma's heart went out to her as she thought of the brutal words Walter and his friends had taunted her with.

After Emma and George left, Roger sat down next to his daughter. "Lauren, Emma means well. She just likes to fix things. She sells books now, but I think she'd also love to hang her social worker shingle on the door."

At that comment, Lauren snorted. "I could sense that right away."

"Honey, you do need to get out from behind the computer. Come with me to Cassandra's next presentation. Or go out with a friend for dinner."

Lauren sighed. She'd heard this so many times before. She truly wanted to have a more normal life. "Okay, Dad. Maybe I'll ask my friend Brenda to have coffee at the bookstore. It'll be like killing two birds with one stone. It would be nice to catch up with her anyway." Lauren hugged her dad, resolved to alleviate his concerns while taking a small step out of her comfort zone.

On Friday evening, Cassandra swept into the bookstore, shining hair curling perfectly around her face. She wore her usual elegant attire, a long skirt with a billowy, feminine blouse and delicate jewelry. Emma always felt dowdy in her presence, so she upped her game with a pretty floral dress and her favorite silver necklace. "Emma, I'm so glad that we'll be continuing. Do you think we will have a good turnout tonight?" Cassandra asked. "Emma, you look lovely tonight."

Emma blushed and thanked Cassandra. "I'm sure we will

have at least six people, maybe more. Janie has made her strawberry scones for us. Good food always brings people in."

When the first attendees arrived, George had just brought the coffee and teapots to the table. Caleb and Rebecca Hill came in, followed by Caroline and Marie, who was warmly greeted by her friends. Next to walk into the café was Roger, who introduced his daughter and her friend, Brenda. Emma was both surprised and delighted that Lauren had accompanied her dad. Janie brought in a box of fragrant scones and brought her mother-in-law, who was also new to the group. Ronnie had expressed interest in hearing about Cassandra's book.

Emma asked the group to take their seats and help themselves to refreshments. Cassandra greeted everyone and hoped their conversation this evening would be enlightening and somewhat light-hearted. One of the chapters of her book dealt with how we would like to be remembered, what she asked everyone at the table to consider. "Think of a short epitaph that could be inscribed to tell the world what you want them to remember about you."

Cassandra glanced briefly at the woman with the facial scar and wondered how she would respond to the assignment. She needn't have worried because Lauren was approaching a turning point. Lauren found that despite her scar and desire for privacy, she had looked forward to visiting the bookstore and participating in a discussion. She hoped she could follow through on her hope to see other people, to be out in the sunshine, to take chances.

After a few moments of scribbling on the paper Cassandra had placed before them, each attendee was ready to share their epitaph. Some were wise (Cal: "He never stopped learning and appreciating the world around him."); some were wistful (Caroline: "She wished she had more time for all the books she hoped to read."); some were funny (Emma: "She put up a valiant fight...but lost." She explained that her family had never had the same need to keep the clean house that she wanted.); and some were sensitive (Lauren: "Her heart was always in the right place.").

After everyone had a chance to share, Cassandra brought out illustrations of unique and humorous epitaphs inscribed on graves she had discovered on the internet. She passed out some examples. "I was hoping for a pyramid," read one stone. Another inscription: "I told you I was sick." "And my favorite," said Cassandra. "Now I can finally rest without that incessant snoring." She explained that she was often tired in the morning because her husband snored.

"This one might be mine because I enjoy baking my own bread," said Rebecca. She giggled as she read the epitaph. "Here Lies John Yeast – Pardon Me For Not Rising."

Emma was delighted that everyone around the table was relaxed and laughing. It was a welcome relief from the more serious "death" discussions.

As the meeting ended, Cassandra outlined the topic she planned for June. "I'm sure you have all heard of birth doulas. Well, recently, there has been interest in people who work as death doulas. We'll be talking about how you feel having someone helping to usher your life out in the way you and your family would want."

Caroline and Marie stayed for a few minutes after everyone else had left. They reviewed last-minute details for a program the library and the bookstore planned to hold together one evening the following week. The program would consist of reading a child's book on owls, followed by a talk by a local ornithologist and a walk around the neighborhood, listening for and hoping to hear an owl's unique hoots. After their return to the store, the children and their parents would be treated to cupcakes Janie baked and decorated like owls. And, of course, there would be an opportunity for the parents and children to browse the bookshelves and make the purchases that kept Moose on the Roof afloat.

The first few weeks in May had been a fun and productive time for the bookstore. The Nielsens looked forward to the end of that weekend and a relaxing Sunday afternoon. George had shopped at a local farm stand and market and picked up a loaf of sourdough bread, cheddar and gouda cheeses, a strawberry rhubarb pie, and a six-pack of local beer. Alfred Hitchcock's *Vertigo*, an old movie starring Jimmy Stewart and Kim Novak was on tap for the evening. Jimmy Stewart had been Emma's dad's favorite movie star, and he was one of Emma's too.

chapter twenty

...

MAY WAS ALSO THE perfect time of year for calves to be born on the Eammons' dairy farm. With warmer weather, increased sunlight, and sufficient grass on the ground, pregnant cows had enough to eat to become strong enough to give birth to healthy calves. Grace had noticed her favorite cow, Moochi, showing signs of coming to term. Her udder was becoming more prominent, and she was acting restless.

On a beautiful, cloudless Saturday morning, Grace and her son, Jesse, visited the barn early to see if Moochi's time had come. The cow was pacing and behaving erratically, alarming mother and son. Walter was away meeting with his distributors for several days, so Grace and Jesse were on their own to bring Moochi's calf into the world. Both had assisted in many births, but Grace felt that the gentle Holstein's behavior was worrying. Without Walter's strength in case Moochi needed an emergency delivery, she had to decide quickly how to help her beloved mother-to-be.

She made a difficult decision as she knelt by Moochi and saw the look of panic in her cow's eyes. Grace looked up at her son.

"Jesse, call Dr Jenkins now. I think Moochi needs a vet. We can't do this on our own. She could die." Grace was beginning to panic as well.

"But, Mom. Dad said..." Jesse was protective of his mother and felt increasingly unsure of himself around his dad.

"I'm not taking any chances. It's her first calf. I know if you call Rand, he will come immediately. Call him...now!" Grace remained with Moochi, trying to keep the cow calm.

Twenty minutes later, Rand arrived in old overalls and boots and assessed the situation. Moochi was lying on her side, panting and shuddering, in obvious distress. The veterinarian pulled on his rubber gloves, and Grace helped lubricate them. Rand kneeled behind the cow and firmly inserted one arm to feel the calf's position in the birth canal. A few minutes later, as he pulled his arm out, two tiny hooves appeared. With practiced expertise, Rand fastened obstetric chains to both hooves and gently pulled on the calf's front legs until, finally, the baby fell onto the soft straw laid down for his birth. Rand sat back on his heels, relieved and grateful that the calf arrived safely. He took his gloves off and wiped the sweat from his brow with a towel Grace gave him.

"Dr Jenkins, here's some water for you." Jesse had thoughtfully brought out bottles of water from the refrigerator. The boy then cleared the calf's nose and mouth and toweled him off. Grace hugged and whispered to her sweet cow as Rand prepared pain medication. This would enable Moochi to stand up, lick her new calf, drink, and feed herself and the calf.

Exhausted and overcome with emotion, Grace stood next to Rand and laid her head on his shoulder. "Thank you, thank you so much for coming. I was petrified Jesse and I would not be able to manage her." She wiped the tears from her eyes with her sleeve.

Aware that Jesse was observing them, Rand stepped gently away from Grace. "I'm very glad you called me, Grace...and Jesse. Moochi should be fine now, but call me if you observe anything off." He gave Grace a bottle of antibiotics and instructions on administering them.

Rand gave Grace's arm a gentle squeeze as he turned to leave. Just then, he looked up and noticed flypaper fluttering from the barn's rafters. "I haven't noticed flypaper in your barn before, Grace. They look old. Where did you get them?"

Grace shrugged. "We found them in an old trunk, probably used by Walter's dad. We've been having such trouble with black flies that we figured they would help temporarily until we found a better solution."

"If you don't mind, I'd like to take one piece back to my clinic and examine it. Old flypaper is laced with arsenic, which is very poisonous to animals...and people. I'll call you to let you know if these are dangerous."

Having composed herself, Grace thanked Rand for helping them with the difficult birth and promised to take down the flypaper if he determined arsenic was present. Rand smiled and nodded to Grace and Jesse. "Take care of that handsome little guy, and call me if Moochi or the calf have any problems."

Grace stood at the head of the driveway, lost in thought, as Rand's truck turned back into Mill River. Jesse was with Moochi and her new calf as Grace approached. "Jesse, you know we had to make a quick decision. Dr Jenkins is our closest vet, and I knew he would come right out. He's a good man."

"Dad will find out, Mom. We can't lie about who helped us." Jesse's stomach was churning thinking about Walter's reaction.

"I know. I'll handle it. It was my decision." Moochi looked tired but content as she licked and encouraged her wobbly calf to stand up. Grace put her arm around Jesse's shoulder. "It's a boy, Jesse. What do you want to name him?"

Jesse beamed at his mom, his blue eyes crinkling. "I've been giving it some thought. Cowabunga. Remember the Teenage Mutant Ninja Turtles? I want to call him Bung for short!"

"Okay, Bung, it is! Now, go tell your sleepyhead sisters they have a new baby to moon over." Grace's heart warmed when she saw her son's exuberance over the birth of a new member of their farm family.

Rand called Grace later that afternoon to let her know that he determined that the flypaper strips did indeed contain traces of arsenic. Even though they were old and the poison had degraded, he advised that she take the strips down and dispose of them appropriately. Grace gave Jesse this job. He put heavy gloves on, climbed a ladder, and reached up to pull down the half dozen strips his parents had hung from the barn's rafters. Being a curious teenager, however, Jesse saved a couple of the strips and put them in a plastic bag to show his buddies in school. "Man," he texted one friend, "I could think of a few teachers I'd use this on. LOL."

In the early evening, Janie dropped by to meet the new calf. "Bung, huh?" Janie playfully ruffled Jesse's hair. "I love it."

"Yup, and you know what Rand found out?" asked Jesse excitedly. "We had poison hanging from the rafters!"

"What? What do you mean?"

"Flypaper strips," explained Grace. "The old ones were made with arsenic to kill the flies. Jesse took them down already."

"Really? Gee, could I have one of those to put in the storage shed? We have mice that have made a nest in there."

"You shouldn't use that anywhere near the restaurant. There's still poison on them," cautioned Grace. Just then, Grace's cell phone rang, and she excused herself to take the call. She had a twinge of panic as she saw the name. It was Walter.

"Aunt Janie, I took two strips of the flypaper," Jesse confessed in a whisper. "One to show my friends and the other, I don't know what for...just...whatever. You can have the other one if you want."

"Uh, sure. Look, we won't mention anything to your mother, but Jess, you must promise to be careful with this stuff, okay?" Janie and Jesse had always had a close relationship.

Grace returned to the barn as Janie pocketed the plastic bag with flypaper. "So, your dad will be back tomorrow, Jesse. Could I have a few minutes with Janie, son?"

Janie was wide-eyed as she looked at her best friend. "Rand was here? What are you going to tell Walter? You're not a good liar."

"I'll tell him it was an emergency and no one else was available. I wasn't going to risk Moochi's life. We have other pregnant heifers and crops to plant. I have to hope Walter will be too busy to get upset about Rand."

"That's naïve, Grace." Janie was seriously worried about Grace's ability to deny the truth about her husband. "The offer always stands. You come to us anytime you feel threatened. Come to dinner soon, anyway. You're skin and bones. We'll put some meat on you."

Grace crossed her arms and leaned her hip against the barn door. She watched as Janie raised one arm in a backward wave as she walked to her truck, her long, trademark braid swinging behind her. Wisps of gray were threaded through her brown hair, and her full-figured curves filled out her denim overalls as she swung her hips comically. Grace laughed out loud. "My best friend, a sexy earth mother." Grace returned to Moochi's stall and looked fondly at her favorite cow and the new calf. She gave them fresh water and hay, administered Moochi's antibiotic, and made sure there was sufficient straw for their bed before returning to the house.

She wanted one more stress-free evening with her children. She knew she had downplayed Walter's likely reaction to Janie. Grace knew there would be hell to pay for what Walter would consider her betrayal. Walter had threatened Rand with bodily harm if he ever set foot on the farm again. As she slowly walked back to the farmhouse, Grace prayed for a solution to her troubled marriage.

Grace discovered the following day that there would be hell to pay. She, however, would not be the only one to pay for it.

chapter twenty-one

. . .

"YOU CAN'T GO IN THERE." Rand's receptionist hurried after the irate man who had just thrown open the entry door, stalked across the small lobby, and forced his way into the examination room. Walter swept the receptionist aside as he approached the veterinarian. He was so focused on Rand that he didn't notice a woman and her dog were also in the room. The dog, startled, leaped off the table, growling and snapping at Walter's ankles. Walter kicked the dog with his heavy boots, shoving him across the floor into the metal table. The dog yelped in pain, and belly to the ground, crawled under the table toward his frightened owner.

Turning his fury on Rand, Walter raised both fists and rained a flurry of abuse on the veterinarian. "I told you to stay off my farm, away from my wife. But you couldn't listen, could you? Well, you will now. I'll have you charged with trespassing. If you don't stay away, I can't be responsible for whatever happens." Walter had become more furious with every word. To Rand's credit, he stoically held his ground, infuriating

Walter even more. The farmer stood threateningly in front of the veterinarian's face.

Walter suddenly became aware of the dog's owner, who was now crouching on the floor, comforting her dog and glaring at Walter with undisguised contempt. He realized it was Roger's daughter, Lauren. "Oh, just perfect. My two favorite people in all of Mill River," he sneered. "Well, fortunate for you that at least your dog loves you. They don't care how ugly you are." When he saw Lauren's face crumple, Walter knew his nasty comment had landed a blow.

Standing protectively in front of Lauren, Rand tried to keep his calm demeanor. "I don't know how to reason with you, Walter. Jesse called me because I was the closest vet available, case closed. You should be relieved they had the foresight not to risk losing one of your animals. So, sure, go ahead and get the police over here. Lauren and I will gladly tell them how you just abused her dog and threatened both of us."

Rand could see that Walter's color was not good and leaned forward to grasp his arm, thinking he might faint. Walter waved him away and backed up a step, seeming to deflate slightly. "All right, I'm going," Walter said in a raspy voice. "But I won't tell you again, Rand. Stay away from my farm and my family." Weakened, but with a final look of disgust, he left the exam room, slamming the door behind him.

Walter barely got to his truck when he collapsed against it, feeling drained and out of breath. Usually, he would take the edge off his anger at his favorite bar, railing against life's wrongs with his like-minded companions. But he couldn't find the energy today. He drove home, parked in front of the barn, and watched his wife and son tending to Moochi and her new calf. He had already berated Grace and Jesse and simply wanted to fall into his recliner with a cold beer.

Berated was not quite the truth. When Walter discovered Rand had helped deliver the calf, he backed Grace up against the sink where she was washing dishes and held her upper arms in a vise. She had cried out in pain, but Walter's mind was in a place where he was beyond reason. When his son tried to intercede on behalf of his mother, Walter angrily pushed him aside, and Jesse fell to the floor. Walter saw fear and confusion in his son's eyes, snapping him back to his senses. Despite his son's response, Walter had resolved to confront Rand. As he drove away from the farmhouse toward town, Walter looked in his rearview mirror. Grace and Jesse were framed in the kitchen door. Grace held her arms protectively around Jesse, whose face was wracked with tears.

Presently, legs up in his recliner, a beer soothing his frayed nerves, Walter continued to justify his behavior. "So, she got roughed up a little. Hell, Grace knew what would happen if I found out about Rand. She'll live. And now the boy learned something, too." As Walter closed his eyes, falling into a troubled sleep, his hand unconsciously covered his heart.

chapter twenty-two
. . .

RAND BENT DOWN TO help Lauren to her feet after the encounter with Walter in the examination room. The dog, a yellow lab named Sandy, who had been there for a yearly check-up, was still cowering under the table.

"Are you okay? I'm so sorry that happened." Rand could see Lauren shaken up and mortified at Walter's continued verbal abuse. "We could report this to the police."

Lauren wiped her eyes with her sleeves and reached for Sandy's collar to help him stand. She bent down to kiss the soft fur of his head, nuzzling him behind his ears to comfort him. "No, please just let this go. We'll be fine. I'd like to get home now if you don't mind. I'll bring Sandy in another day, okay?" And with that, Lauren hurried out of the office, ignoring the curious and concerned faces of those in the waiting room.

Rand took a few moments to assure them and his receptionist that they had nothing to worry about. Somehow, he got through the next two hours until the end of his work day. Rand drove home and slowly walked up his front steps, taking a moment to sit on his porch swing. He leaned forward with his elbows resting on his knees and looked toward Grace and Walter's farm, deep in thought. Walter had been verbally threatening and had hurt Lauren's dog, but she had not wanted to involve the town's police department. Walter had friends there, and Rand did not think they would do anything more than have a cordial chat with the farmer.

He had to admit to himself that he was relieved. He did not want to hurt Grace by making Walter angrier by calling the police. He also wondered why Walter became pale and backed off so quickly.

Lauren and Sandy walked the short distance to the pharmacy. When Lauren saw her father, she could no longer hold back the tears. Roger put his arm around Lauren and guided her to the back room, where he asked his daughter what had happened.

Lauren told him about Walter and what he'd done, including humiliating her. "I've been trying, Dad. I do want to be out with people instead of hiding away here. But Walter...Oh, God, will he ever leave me alone? He suddenly seems to be everywhere!"

Roger listened intently. "You know, it's almost closing time. I'm going to put the 'Closed' sign on the door, and we are going out to dinner. I want you to get washed up. You need some of Janie's and Mike's home cooking. Go ahead now; I'll feed Sandy." Roger tried to put on a cheerful face, but inside, he was fuming.

While Lauren freshened up, Roger stood at the counter, hands balled into fists at his side. How he would love to smash one of those fists into Walter's repugnant face. He knew, however, that provoking the man was like poking a snake with a stick. Roger stood at the counter, his mind at work, until he saw Lauren emerge from the back room. "You look a hundred times better, sweetie. Come on, let's go eat!"

Janie asked her mother-in-law to take her place at the restaurant that evening. While Walter slept, Jesse called her to tell her what happened when his dad discovered Rand helped birth Moochi's calf. Infuriated that Walter had pushed his son and once again assaulted Grace, she was intent on convincing the family to get into her truck and leave the farm. She drove as quickly as she could, images of Walter abusing his family crowding out any other thoughts in her mind.

Janie and Grace stood in the kitchen, talking quietly. Janie gestured urgently for Grace and her children to leave the house quickly. Neither of them noticed Walter as he approached the entryway. "What's going on here? Some secret meeting of the girls?" Walter's voice was sarcastic, but his stance was threatening.

Hands on her hips, Janie approached Walter and looked him in the eye. "I want Grace and the kids to come with me now. You've put your hands on her for the last time. And what kind of man pushes his own son down?" Wary, Janie was ready for Walter's angry response and was confused when it didn't come.

Walter ignored Janie, appealing directly to Grace. "Okay, I had a rough week. I was exhausted from traveling all over the state. I'm sorry. I promise it will never happen again. Look, I'm serious. How about we get those goats you've been wanting? Make cheese, sell goat milk, or do whatever you want. I love you, Grace. Please, let's start fresh."

Janie wasn't buying any of Walter's promises. "Grace," she said softly. "You know abusers don't change. I speak from experience, you know that."

Grace was quietly listening to both her husband and her best friend. She was taken aback by how pale and drawn Walter appeared. Was he so frightened she would leave? Could this possibly be a turning point? Grace looked beseechingly at Janie. "I know you're looking out for me, Janie. But I want my family and my home. I'm going to stay and hold Walter to his promises. My children love this farm. I'm needed here, by them, and by my animals."

Walter stepped to his wife's side, smugly putting an arm around her shoulder. He didn't notice Grace flinched slightly, but Janie did. "Okay, Grace," she said softly, stepping away. "But, Walter, I have my eyes on you. So does Mike." Shaking her head, Janie made one more appeal to Grace. When there was no response, she took a few steps back, turned around, and walked out the back door to her truck.

The following day, the town's gossip mill was going full force. Everyone knew that Walter had barged into Rand's office, threatened him, and lashed out at Lauren. The town's sympathy was not on Walter's side.

Emma and George had dinner with June and Rob in their private quarters at the inn in the evening. Over a casual dinner of the inn's signature tomato bisque, they speculated about the incident and why Grace would choose to remain with a man who was physically abusive to her. He had begun to harm his son as well.

"Grace loves that farm," Emma sighed. "And maybe she is frightened of how Walter would respond if she took the kids from him. What's that expression? It's better to stay with the devil you know?"

June added, "I don't think his behavior is predictable in any event, whether she stays or goes."

"He's a narcissist," said Rob, unable to hide the contempt in his voice. "God help her if she openly defies him."

George held his tongue. As a former police officer, he saw the tragic result of many abusive relationships.

Father Cal and Rebecca had heard from several folks about what happened in the veterinarian's office. Janie, fearing for Grace's safety, had called him for advice. The couple prayed and talked about what they should do. Cal drove to the farm and asked if Walter and Grace would return to the parsonage with him for a late dinner. In the meantime, Rebecca put on some soup, made a quick batch of biscuits, and placed butter and a salad on the table. Walter was reluctant to air their dirty laundry and balked at first. However, he agreed, if only to keep Grace on the farm...where he could keep a suspicious eye on her.

With Grace's encouragement, Walter grudgingly agreed to a weekly counseling session. Cal felt that there was no time like the present, so he took both of their hands. "Why don't we get started?" he gently said.

chapter twenty-three

. . .

EMMA STEPPED ONTO HER patio holding a steaming cup of coffee, appreciating the morning sun sparkling through the tall maples in her backyard. After a tumultuous May, June had finally arrived in Vermont, and the days were pleasantly warm. Vacationers were arriving with luggage and canoes perched on top of their SUVs. Roadside farm stands were popping up like dandelions. The last of the snow trickled down mountain peaks, swelling the river running through the town.

This morning, George was already in the garden preparing the soil for the perennials and annuals he purchased the previous day. Emma saw black-eyed susans, zinnias, dahlias, and marigolds. There were brilliant red geraniums, which Emma wanted to place in terracotta pots on the patio. George was erecting a trellis, against which he would plant one of Emma's favorite flowers, sky-blue morning glories. Some hardy flowers were already serving as a dramatic backdrop, where the garden was shaded by towering pines and maples: hosta and foxglove, both with lavender bell-shaped blossoms that hummingbirds loved. George had also purchased two hummingbird feeders, one for each side of the garden, for the tiny, territorial birds.

"Remember to rest and drink enough water," Emma called to George. "I'm heading to the bookstore. And don't forget that Maggie is coming over the weekend. She can help with the garden, too."

"Don't worry. I'll take breaks. I'll order pizza and a Greek salad for dinner, okay?"

Emma drove along the highway into Mill River, enjoying the wildflowers waving in the light breeze. She stopped at The Down Home Grill to pick up Janie's blueberry muffins and chocolate chip cookies. In a couple of hours, a class of boisterous first-graders would visit Moose on the Roof Books for a lesson on local wildlife.

Marie and Caroline helped Emma select age-appropriate books about animals native to Vermont, and a local environmentalist would talk to them about beavers, bats, bears, chipmunks, voles, deer, and, of course, moose. Emma would send each child home with a picture book. Parents who attended were free to browse the shelves of books and gather in the café for coffee and muffins or cookies.

Maggie arrived Friday night, and after talking about what was new with her job, she casually mentioned a new boyfriend. Emma's ears perked up, and she asked, "Anything serious?" Emma could never stop hoping that both of her children would settle down. But to her everlasting consternation, both Maggie and Jack would look at her and say: "Mom, leave it be!"

Changing the subject abruptly, Maggie asked her father what he needed help with in the garden. "How about we make sure the trellis is stable, and you can help rake some compost into the flower bed? After that, we could have lunch in Manchester. Just the two of us since Mom will be working tomorrow."

"That sounds great, Dad." She gave her mother a sidelong glance. "And I'll tell you all about that guy I'm dating. I think he may be the one." Maggie winked conspiratorially at George and hugged her mom. "You never know, Mom," Maggie sang, drawing out her words.

When Emma returned home Saturday evening, she found Maggie grilling chicken. A salad and fresh biscuits were already on the table. "Hi, sweetie," Emma called from the back door. "Your father's usually the grill master. Where is he?"

"Chicken's almost done. Can you pour a couple of glasses of wine? I'll be right in."

Maggie had not answered her question, but Emma figured George was probably napping on the couch. She put plates and silverware on the table, set three glasses out for white wine, and patted Annie, who twined herself around Emma's legs, wanting attention. Maggie walked in, carrying the serving dish and setting it on the table. She took a long drink of wine and sighed. "Dad's resting in the bedroom. I think he overdid it today. Why don't we have dinner? We'll talk about it afterward, okay? Let's let him sleep."

Emma let any concern slip from her mind as they ate and caught up on the doings in their lives. Afterward, they took their cups of tea to the patio and enjoyed the sunset, the sky turning slowly from pink and purple to a deep blue that matched the morning glories. Maggie was finally ready to talk. A look of worry clouded her sweet face. "Dad lost his balance on the way to the restaurant. If I weren't right there, he would have fallen.

Then, at lunch, he told me he saw Aunt Jenny in the garden yesterday. He says he forgot to tell you. She was picking flowers. And then, when he took another look, she was no longer there. Mom, he knows that Jenny is in Manhattan, but he also swears that he saw her! It really upset me."

"I know that Dad has been having more difficulty with Parkinson's. Dr Shah increased his medication and said he could have more hallucinations as a result." Emma felt awful that her daughter had seen her father's most upsetting symptoms. She reached out to hug her daughter.

Just then, however, Maggie noticed her dad standing at the French doors to the patio, looking tired and annoyed. "I did see Jenny. I know it's not logical, but I saw her." He stalked back into the kitchen.

Emma got up to soothe her husband. "Remember what Dr Shah said? Come on, sit on the patio with Maggie, and I'll heat a plate of chicken for you."

After a while, George's hurt feelings dissipated, and he relaxed. After dessert, Maggie collected the cups and dishes and put them in the dishwasher. She remained at the French doors, looking out at her parents and the darkening sky. It saddened her to see her dad, who had been so strong all his life, become older and vulnerable. She wished she could stay a few more days in Vermont but needed to return to her job on Long Island.

Emma's concern about George notwithstanding, she also had to attend to their business. She decided to ask George to accompany her to the bookstore more often. There was always something that needed fixing: shelves to be stocked, coffee pots to be washed and refilled. On Tuesday, George felt more like himself, and they drove into town together. He brought a large bouquet of foxglove, which he placed in a sturdy vase between the two armchairs on the table. Afterward, he made the coffee and a pot of boiling water for tea. Janie arrived with oatmeal raisin cookies and butter croissants.

"Hi, Emma. I'll just put these...." Janie suddenly stopped short in front of the vase of foxglove. She frowned and seemed to hesitate, considering what to say. "Emma, do you know that foxglove is poisonous? If your customers touch or smell those flowers, they can get a nasty rash, or worse."

"I didn't know. George brought it in from our garden. He's been wearing gloves, so I guess they protected his hands."

"Yeah, the gloves probably helped. If you really want to keep them in the store, you should put the vase on the shelf behind the register."

"I will, Janie. Thanks for looking out." Emma took a second look at the younger woman. "Are you feeling all right? Your face is flushed." Instinctively, Emma reached out to feel Janie's forehead. Janie stepped back abruptly, putting her hand up to block Emma.

"I'm fine," said Janie, quickly walking back to the café and dropping the boxes on the table. Head down, Janie practically ran out the door, calling to Emma that she would be back on Friday. She got into her truck and looked at herself in the rearview mirror. She put her hands to her cheeks, which were red and hot to the touch. "Oh, Lord! How stupid can I be?" She knocked her head on the steering wheel a couple of times and groaned in frustration.

Emma put the flowers behind the register and explained why to George. She looked out the front door as Janie's truck spun its wheels and took off. "I'll never understand her. Even when that girl is being nice, she's still prickly. She just took off like a bat out of Hell." Emma wondered if their icy relationship would ever thaw.

It was a slow morning, with just a trickle of customers. Emma had time to open boxes, fill orders, and prepare for Cassandra's next program, scheduled for Friday night. She wondered if the confrontation in Rand's office and the gossip around town would affect who and how many people would turn up. Or would the scuttlebutt bring spectators hoping to see some symbolic blood spilled?

chapter twenty-four
...

ON FRIDAY EVENING, EMMA had reason to pray for an uneventful meeting. Father Cal had called earlier to discuss bringing Grace and Walter. "I don't want to create a problem, Emma, but I've been working with both of them, and they would like to remain part of the community. They understand they are the topic of much speculation and want to confront any antagonism head-on."

"You are all welcome here, Cal," Emma said. "If Roger and Rand are here, I can't vouch for how they will react. But anything that will keep Grace connected is fine with me. I know she has been enjoying these evenings."

In addition to the "regulars," there was a librarian friend of Marie and Caroline and the twenty-something daughter of Brenda, Lauren's friend. The daughter, Amy, was about to start medical school and thought she could learn something from the discussion. Cal and Rebecca arrived with Walter and Grace in tow as everyone took their seats. Emma noticed Roger's cheeks were flush with anger. Rand's eyes were wary and full of concern. To their credit, however, they were both gentlemen and remained seated and silent, choosing not to cause any disruption.

Grace's eyes flitted back and forth nervously as she looked at the people seated around the table. Emma saw her glance through lowered lashes at Rand. Walter seemed pale and subdued, and Emma wondered if he was ill or simply ill at ease.

Cassandra cleared her throat, and everyone stopped talking. "I'd like to welcome you all. I see a couple of newcomers. I want you both to feel free to join the discussion. We all have opinions about the subject matter, and there is no judgment at this table. It's important to respect each other's thoughts. This evening, I want to present the concept of hiring a death doula. She or he helps facilitate the kind of death that a client and their family would want."

Cassandra explained how much or how little a doula would be present, the legacies they could help their client and family create, and how the doula prepares their clients physically, emotionally, and spiritually for death. "The doulas run their own business, and a contract outlines exactly what services the doula can offer and what the clients want. So, let's open up the discussion to how you all would feel about this service."

As usual, Father Cal opened the discussion. "'Service' seems like such an impersonal word. It's interesting that death now requires an outsider, a contract, and a fee. Years ago, family was always present when someone was dying. But now, families live all over the country or the world. It's sad to have to hire someone to help you in the dying process."

Amy added her point of view as a prospective physician: "It's caused by the depersonalization of medical care as well. People don't want to die in a sterile hospital or nursing home.

It's only in recent years that doctors are taught about the emotional and spiritual aspects of death and dying."

June, the former nurse, also weighed in: "I've known a couple of death doulas. They tend to be quite empathetic and in tune with the family and patient. They can help bridge the awkwardness of what to say and do for someone considered terminal. I agree, though, that signing a contract and hiring someone seems impersonal."

As Grace added her opinion, she blushed, never quite sure that her opinion was valid. "I think I would welcome a death doula. Living on a farm, death is a natural occurrence to me. But I think my children would have a hard time dealing if one of us was dying. If a doula could help them cope, I'm all for it."

Emma glanced at Walter, who seemed impatient and skeptical of the discussion. Rolling his eyes, he leaned back in his chair and crossed his arms as if disassociating himself from the group. Although none of the attendees had any personal experience with death doulas, almost everyone had an opinion. Emma noticed, however, that Roger and Rand were uncharacteristically quiet. It was clear neither of them was quite comfortable with Walter present.

Janie suddenly rushed in and brought a much-needed distraction. She apologized for her late arrival and quickly set out classic and triple chocolate chip cookies. Emma and George poured coffee and tea, and the people around the table dug in and seemed more relaxed as they shared Janie's delicious dessert.

Emma announced that there would be no meeting next month because she and George would be taking a vacation, and they would resume in August. As the meeting broke up,

Emma observed Walter glaring at Rand and Roger. He seemed to understand, however, that he dared not do or say anything to create a disturbance. Father Cal was immediately aware of the uneasiness between the three men and put his arm around Walter's shoulder, both in support and warning, as they walked out to their cars. Rebecca slipped her arm through Grace's and said good night as well.

June, Cassandra, and Emma remained at the table after everyone had gone home. George busied himself in the office perusing a book about gardening.

Emma let out a pent-up breath. "That went better than I thought it would. I'm so glad Grace feels comfortable here. But did either of you notice that Walter doesn't look healthy?"

"He certainly doesn't," said June. "I know he has a heart condition, but he must be stressed as well. He likes to be in control of everything, and I think right now, he sees that he is not. I can see the parsonage from the inn, and I'm glad Cal has taken Walter and Grace under his wing." June had known Walter for many years and expressed uncertainty that counseling would make a difference in Walter's behavior in the long run.

"He is holding in his anger and not doing a very good job of it," Cassandra added in her formal way of speaking. "Perhaps that is adding to his physical distress. I can see that this is a man whose rage will make him explode one day." She threw her arms out dramatically as if simulating an explosion. "I hope his wife and children are far from him when he does."

The three friends sat there in silence, each absorbing Cassandra's prediction's implications.

chapter twenty-five
. . .

THE TOWNSPEOPLE OF MILL River celebrated July Fourth on the expansive field at The Grange. There were speeches by local politicians, lawn games, fireworks, and lots of food. The convenience store in town provided hot dogs and buns with all the fixings. June and Rob brought the Mill River Inn's famous barbecued ribs and cornbread. Janie and Mike closed their restaurant for the day and brought several varieties of pie. Walter and Grace brought coolers of ice cream made with cream from their dairy cows. Families volunteered to bring all manner of salads for the shared table.

In public, Walter behaved like a loving husband and father. Despite the couple's counseling sessions with Father Cal, Walter privately continued to be suspicious and angry with Grace and Jesse, by whom he felt betrayed. Their daughters were too young to understand the underlying tensions between their parents. They wanted to love both their mom and dad. Jesse, however, remained hostile to his father after Walter viciously hurt his mother and pushed him to the kitchen floor.

Walter refused to listen to Jesse's plea that they were concerned about Moochi's delivering a dead calf or possibly dying during the birth herself. Since then, Jesse avoided his father or pointedly ignored him. In response, Walter never missed an opportunity to criticize Jesse's work around the farm. Now, seeing Walter hypocritically playing the perfect dad as he dished out ice cream cones and playfully bantered with all the children at the picnic, Jesse felt disgusted.

Walking over to the edge of the field by the tree line, Jesse pulled the plastic bag with the flypaper strip out of his jeans pocket and sat in the shade of an oak tree. He felt powerless. As he considered the flypaper, he wondered if he could scrape some particles from the surface. Maybe put it on some food and see what happens. He knew his father had not been looking well recently. Would a few grains of arsenic do anything? Glancing around first to see if anyone was coming, Jesse took out his pocket knife and scraped some grains off the flypaper into the plastic bag. Jesse was fourteen years old. His anger and impulsiveness had taken hold.

Snapping off a large leaf from the tree, Jesse wrapped the flypaper in it before tucking it into his back pocket. He walked over to the food table, grabbed a hot dog, put some relish and mustard on it the way Walter liked, and surreptitiously mixed some of the grains from the flypaper with a coffee stirrer. "Hey, Dad," Jesse smiled coyly as he walked over to Walter. "How about a hot dog? I made it how you like it."

Walter was surprised but was hot and sweaty from serving ice cream and figured his son was trying to make an overture. "Sure, thanks. Hey, it looks good, Son." He patted Jesse on the back, winking at a group of children patiently waiting for cups of ice cream. Walter practically stuffed the whole hot dog into his mouth in one bite. A second later, he spat it out, gagging at the bitter taste. "What the hell was in that thing? What did you do?" Walter hovered over his son as Jesse backed up, arms in front of him, trying to ward off a blow. The group of children, frightened, scattered.

Grace and Cal ran over and interjected themselves between father and son.

"He put something funny in that hot dog," Walter bellowed. "Get me a beer. I've got to get that taste out of my mouth." He continued gagging and spitting until Grace handed him a beer, and he took a good long drink. "I'll deal with you later," he hissed at his son. "Don't think I'll forget this." He hovered menacingly over Jesse.

"Walter, please stop," Grace begged. "Come sit with me in the shade. I'll fix you another plate." Grace was desperate. She didn't know what her son did but feared for him. She pleaded that Walter remain with her until he calmed down.

Janie had been quietly observing the altercation. She pulled Jesse away from the party and asked him what happened. Sheepishly, Jesse pulled the leaf from his pocket and showed her the flypaper.

"Geez, I had a feeling you were going to pull some stupid prank. What were you thinking? Listen, I'm not going to say anything, okay? But you need to get rid of that...now! When we're done here, Mike and I will drive to the farm to check on you all. You know your dad won't let this go."

"I know it was stupid, but Aunt Janie, I hate what he's done to us, especially to my mom. I wish he would die," he said softly. He looked at Janie, his freckled face blotchy and stained with tears. He collapsed, sobbing, against Janie's shoulder, his body shaking.

"I know, Jesse. I know." Janie hugged the young boy fiercely, wiping a few tears from her own eyes. "He doesn't deserve any of you."

The ride back to the Eammons' farm was tense. Grace and Jesse avoided looking at each other. Both could see that Walter was in a silent rage. Pulling into the driveway and parking, Walter calmly...too calmly...eased out of the car and unlocked the house's front door. The twins, sensing trouble, decided to visit the cows and the newly purchased goats in the enclosure by the barn. Walter held the door open, gesturing to Grace and Jesse to enter, his face an unreadable mask. As soon as they did, Walter turned wildly on them.

Walter took Jesse by the shoulder, digging his fingers into the soft, fleshy area under the clavicle. "You trying to make me sick, boy?" Jesse tried to slip away from his father's grasp, but Walter pushed him against the wall. Jesse looked at his mother, silently imploring her to stay away. Grace, meanwhile, stood against the kitchen drawer where she had stashed a large shard of glass last Thanksgiving. She surreptitiously reached for it and concealed it behind her back.

Grace was a lioness, where her children were concerned. She put her hand on Walter's arm to pull him away, but he swung around and backhanded her across the face. His ring opened a gash on her cheek, and as she automatically put her hand up to cover her cheek, the shard clattered to the floor. Walter stood in front of her in disbelief. Grace cried out and reached for a towel to stanch the blood beginning to drip down her face. Walter picked up the glass and held it in front of his wife.

He smirked. "Congratulations," he said coolly, pocketing the shard. "I didn't think you had it in you. As for your dear son, what would your precious Father Cal say about a boy trying to poison his own father? That's what it was, wasn't it?" Walter turned toward Jesse. He looked like an animal about to attack his prey. Jesse was still hunched in the corner of the kitchen, hatred marring his young face.

Grace was shaking, but she gathered her courage and stood her ground. "He would say that you are an abusive thug!"

Just as Walter loomed menacingly over his petite wife, Janie and Mike arrived at the kitchen door. Mike shouted, distracting Walter. "Get away from her, Walter. We're taking Grace and the kids with us. You need time to simmer down. I'll be back for whatever they need to stay with us for a few days." Janie put her arms around Grace and Jesse and led them out of the kitchen.

"I'll get the girls, too." She didn't realize that Lizabeth and Ellie, having heard the commotion, were already standing at the threshold, eyes wide with fear, their arms around each other.

Walter looked around the kitchen at his twins and at Mike, who was standing in front of him, muscular arms crossed, ready for any confrontation. Walter shook his head wearily and backed away. He was breathing heavily at this point. Sinking into his easy chair, he waved his hand as if to dismiss everyone. He set his jaw, eyes straight ahead, his body finally at rest.

chapter twenty-six

. . .

ON JULY FOURTH, EMMA and George were also enjoying games, barbecue, and fireworks. They, their two children, and George's sister, Jennifer, were celebrating their thirty-fifth wedding anniversary with a week at their favorite Pocono Mountain resort. They'd left a scowling Annie with June and Rob at the Inn.

George was relaxing in a lawn chair, reading a book, and reaching for a cold lemonade when he noticed Emma and Jennifer at the edge of the lawn, fawning over the bed of colorful summer flowers. As Emma bent over to sniff an heirloom rose, George chuckled. "Hmmm, she still has that shapely bottom I remember from all those years ago."

As he gazed at the two women, he realized that Jennifer reminded him of someone. Somehow, it seemed important to remember, but the answer kept dancing around the edges of his memory. There were times when a sort of brain fog set in these days. George wasn't someone to fret over his physical limitations since his diagnosis of Parkinson's, but thinking about losing his memory troubled him greatly.

Distracted by his attempt to jump-start his memory, George was startled when Maggie and Jack, wrapped in towels after a swim, suddenly appeared at his side. "The barbecue is ready," announced an always-ravenous Jack. "Come on, the food looks amazing." And it was. The family chose a picnic table in the shade and settled in for hamburgers, barbecued chicken, coleslaw, and macaroni salad. Apple crumb pie and vanilla ice cream was a perfect dessert.

After talking about all the activities they had been participating in and all the resort's ample offerings of food, Maggie sighed. "I'm so relaxed...and full. I hate to go home." Raising her cup of coffee, Emma proposed a toast to her family. "To the best family we could ever have. Why don't we do this every year?"

And so it was agreed.

Emma and George were happy to return to their little cottage in Mill River and to reunite with their furry little girl. "I can see Annie didn't lose any weight," Emma noted when she picked her up from the Inn. I guess she wasn't pining for us."

"Actually, Oliver and Annie became buddies after some hissing and hiding under couches," said June. "Oliver's quite a bit younger, so Annie treated him like a kitten. They were so cute together."

Emma was happy to get back to the bookstore as well. The following morning, she picked up a couple of muffins and coffee at the convenience store and parked in front of The Moose, as she liked to call the bookstore. Sure enough, the crows greeted her with manic caws. "Okay, I got the message. I got a muffin for you guys, too." She threw some crumbs in the backyard and unlocked the door to the store. She noticed

Father Cal in front of the church, heading toward her. She waved. "Come on in. I'll share my coffee and muffin with you."

He reached the doorstep, glancing up to see the crows flying off for their breakfast. "Hey, Emma. I see the birds missed their benefactor!"

"Ha! I guess I'm just a soft touch. Would you like to share?" Emma said, holding up the coffee and muffin.

"No thanks. I just had some of Rebecca's homemade raisin bread. You look relaxed. I trust you enjoyed your vacation."

"Just what the doctor ordered. So, how are things here?"

Cal updated Emma on all the happenings in town, ending with the scene at the July Fourth picnic: "Grace, Jesse, and the twins are staying with Ronnie. She has a big, old, rambling house. I think Grace is itching to get back to the farm, though. She misses her animals and wants to make sure they're all right."

"Are she and Jesse going to be safe? Did anyone figure out what was in the hot dog?"

"No. Jesse is mum. But if he did put something in it, there are lots of things on a farm that could be dangerous. I'm trying to work with Grace and Walter, and I hoped they wouldn't have to separate, but Walter needed to calm down. He also needs to stop drinking and to see his doctor, but I wouldn't hold my breath for him to do any of that."

"Thanks for letting me know," Emma said. "I hope Grace can get back to her animals...safely. She's been looking forward to raising goats. She told me about her dream of making enough cheese for a side business."

"I hope so, too. Mike and Janie will also be keeping an eye on them. And you know Janie. She can be fierce."

"I've surely seen that side of her," Emma agreed.

"Well, I'll let you catch up with work, Emma. I've got a sermon to write."

She said goodbye to Cal and then walked into the main part of her bookstore. "Okay, now to get to work."

She decided to set up a table with books about presidents. After all, stories about success, scandal, and sedition at the highest level of government sold well. She decorated the table with red, white, and blue bunting and would ask George to cut flowers from their garden to put in a vase on the table. The month of July would bring in vacationers to the store. She put out a few games for children to play with while their parents browsed the shelves.

Emma's friends were also vacationing or hosting visitors. Cassandra was in Greece with her husband. Rand's parents had traveled from northern Vermont to stay with him, and Roger seemed to be spending more time away from the town at his cabin in the mountains. Emma and June carved out time to have coffee together a couple of times a week. June let Emma know that Grace, despite that terrible scene in the kitchen, had quietly returned to the farm. Cal had his misgivings and urged the couple to continue their counseling sessions.

Emma was pleasantly surprised when Grace briefly stopped at the bookstore to tell her how much the cheesemaking book had helped her. Emma felt Grace's manner was somewhat subdued, and she couldn't help noticing a large bandage on her friend's cheek. It was apparent Grace did not want to talk further. After leaving the bookstore, she walked up the street to the pharmacy to pick up Walter's medication refills.

In Roger's absence, Lauren waited on Grace. She didn't know what to think as she took Grace's measure. The woman's husband was cruel, yet Grace returned to him. Inwardly, Lauren shrugged. *She made her bed. Now she has to lie in it*, she thought. She had not forgotten Walter's abuse in the veterinarian's office.

Toward the end of the month, Janie made another of her frequent visits to the Eammons' farm to check on the family. The household seemed quiet...too quiet. Grace walked on tenterhooks around her husband. Jesse kept to himself unless he was doing chores. Walter roamed around the house like a caged tiger, increasingly isolated from his family in his own home. Janie shuddered and wondered when the tension would come to a head.

It was sooner than she would have thought.

Grace stood at the kitchen sink washing dishes one hot and steamy evening after dinner. She swept the tendrils of her strawberry blonde hair away from her face, and her cheeks were a lovely rosy hue. Walter sat at the kitchen table drinking beer, contemplating his beautiful wife. He stood somewhat unsteadily and approached Grace from behind. As he caressed her shoulders and bent to kiss her neck, she stiffened. "What are you doing?" Grace asked uneasily.

Immediately feeling rejected, Walter sputtered. "Y-you're my wife. I'm not allowed to touch you now? What good is talking to that pastor if we can't get along? Answer me!"

"You're scaring me, Walter." Grace stepped to the side so that Walter could not push her into the counter. "It takes time. I...I can't give you an answer right now. Please don't pressure me." Grace felt as if she was shrinking into herself.

"Oh, but I bet you could give Rand an answer, couldn't you?" Scowling, his face flushed not only from the heat but also from several beers, he grasped her upper arms tightly, digging his fingers in. Grace knew there would be purple bruises by morning. Walter opened his mouth to continue berating Grace for avoiding what he considered her marital duty. Suddenly, though, his breathing became ragged, and he staggered backward, falling heavily into the kitchen chair.

Alarmed, Grace filled a glass with cold water and brought it to him.

"Just leave me alone. I need to catch my breath, that's all." Walter dismissed her.

And Grace backed out of the kitchen, wondering, hoping, dreading. There were too many conflicting emotions swirling in her head.

chapter twenty-seven
. . .

THE DOG DAYS OF August crept into the valley between the Green and Taconic Mountains. People in canoes and inner tubes meandered lazily along the Mill River. Farmers' markets were brimming with a summer's bounty of produce. Flower gardens overflowed with large clusters of blue or pink hydrangeas, daylilies, marigolds, zinnias, and sunflowers. George's backyard garden was a sight to behold. The blue morning glories were a stunning border along the trellis. Emma admired the garden every morning as she took her coffee out onto the patio and watched the morning glories unfurl their petals to the sun.

George had agreed to accompany Emma to work more often after Maggie's weekend visit. Emma discovered many minor repairs that could keep her husband busy. His current project was shoring up a few wobbly steps leading to the bell tower and touching up the grout in the stone walls. Emma was in no rush to finish the job, so George took his time. He enjoyed taking care of the café, refilling coffee pots, and chatting with friends and visitors alike. Emma found that he was an excellent emissary for "The Moose."

Cassandra called to let Emma know she had returned to Bennington and would be available to continue her monthly programs. They set a date for the third Friday evening in August.

The Eammons remained in the farmhouse together in a tense standoff. Neither of them seemed inclined to break up the family, and Grace was especially motivated to stay since her goats were now giving milk, and she was beginning to experiment with producing cheese. Jesse and the twins would be starting school in September, and Grace was determined that they would stay in the same school with the friends and activities they were accustomed to. Cal continued to counsel Grace and Walter but was discovering that their relationship was likely fatally damaged.

Janie visited Grace often. They brought their coffee and the muffins or scones Janie baked to the picnic table and talked about their lives, current and past. Janie seemed more willing to talk about the emotional and physical abuse she had witnessed growing up in her home in West Virginia. She talked lovingly about the grandmother who took her under her wing. Grace spoke of her childhood on a cooperative farm, where children seemed to be communal property. Parents were busy simply trying to survive on a limited amount of money, but Grace recalled the adults somehow found enough to purchase beer and marijuana. "Janie, I didn't feel like I belonged there. I wanted a real home and family. Something I could call just my own."

"I know what you mean," Janie said quietly. "A place where people were kind to each other. Where I could feel secure." She looked toward the pasture, tending to be shy when revealing anything of herself. Neither woman had ever had a close girlfriend, so their friendship brought both much-needed comfort.

"Gosh, are we getting sentimental." Grace laughed. "Why don't we toast?" She clinked her coffee mug against Janie's. "Friends forever!"

In a bow to the "Dog Days," Emma set her display table with books about dogs and astronomy. The link was the Dog Star, Sirius. Emma and the librarians arranged a night of star gazing through telescopes provided by an astronomer from Bennington College. Rand, Roger, and Cal brought their gentle, kid-friendly dogs for the children to pet.

The third Friday in August dawned oppressively hot and humid. Wisps of fog from the cool mountain tops floated, ghost-like, across the fields. This meant a busy day inside the air-conditioned bookshop. By the time Emma and George closed up that evening, they were ready for a quick dinner at home.

As they pulled into the driveway, Emma glimpsed Annie with her pink nose glued to the front window, looking frantic for her dinner. Annie missed the snacks that soft-hearted George fed her when he was home. Even though her tummy was full after Emma gave her her favorite beef and vegetable cat food, she still circled George's legs, sniffing the aroma of leftover fried chicken as George set the table.

The couple ate quickly, freshened up, and got back into the car for the return trip to Moose on the Roof. Cassandra would be arriving shortly for her Friday night program. Emma brought a couple of leftover buttermilk biscuits to toss to 'her' crows. She was amused by their gifts of bottle caps, twigs, and shiny pieces of glass. "I don't know what you find so fascinating about them." George shuddered whenever he walked past the oily-looking birds.

"They're very intelligent. I read recently that in ancient times, they were associated with Apollo, the Greek God of prophecy," argued Emma. "I like how they seem to watch over our shop."

"I've heard that they're bad luck," George said crossly, with a 'so, there' look on his face. Emma looked at him with raised eyebrows. As George walked into the bookstore to begin preparation for the evening's program, Emma held back. She crumbled the biscuits for a few crows milling about on the grass. One loud squawk made her look up to the roof. The most prominent crow was standing sentry over the arched doorway, one black eye cocked towards her. Emma suddenly felt chilled, and she walked quickly into the bookstore.

George filled the coffee pot while Emma lit several calming sage candles before placing plates and mugs on the table. Cassandra strode in wearing a gauzy top and long-swirly skirt, her hair loose and wavy. Emma smiled to herself when she saw George take an appreciative look.

The 'regulars' started arriving a few minutes later. Marie and Caroline complimented Emma on her 'star and dog' display of books. June and George chatted about the Nielsens' recent vacation. Roger entertained Rand and Cassandra with a long story about catching a giant fish, his arms spread wide. Emma could see humorous but doubtful expressions on both their faces.

All eyes went to the doorway when Cal and Rebecca accompanied Walter to a chair at the old pine café table. Rebecca explained that Grace was tending to one of the twins, who was home with a fever. The group gathered in the cafe could accept that Cal, as a minister, was motivated to help Walter become a person the community could trust. However, not everyone was inclined to feel that Walter deserved that opportunity.

Cassandra leaned forward and asked for everyone's attention. "Tonight, let's talk about The Conversation. Has anyone ever heard of that expression?" June and Emma nodded their heads. "There is an initiative called The Conversation Project. The aim is to help everyone talk about their wishes for care through the end of life, in other words, to be understood and respected. This is a difficult conversation for some people. It's best to talk about these things when you are well and before a medical crisis. Think about someone with a terminal illness… or end-stage Alzheimer's who cannot communicate their wishes. Has anyone had this conversation or been in the kind of situation I just mentioned?"

Roger took a deep breath and then described the conversations he and his wife had after she was diagnosed with cancer. "I wish we had discussed what Marjorie wanted before her diagnosis. But even though it was painful, we became closer as we talked about the future and what kind of treatment she would tolerate. She decided to stop treatment a few months before she died, and although it was heart-rending, I supported her choice."

"When I was working, there was a woman who had emergency surgery for a twisted colon," Emma said. "She was old and frail, and the surgery left her non-responsive and on a ventilator. At first, the family agreed she should be taken off the vent, but after she was, her husband demanded it be put back in. The family seemed to be in crisis until we looked at her Living Will, and there in black and white was her wish not to be kept alive artificially. People make these legal documents but don't talk it through to ensure their family understands the importance of those words."

"That's so true," Cal said, interjecting. "I counsel many families who have no idea what their loved one wants. They are left to make decisions that make them feel guilty and unsure."

And June spoke emotionally about her mother, who had always made it clear that she wanted no ventilators, feeding tubes, or cardiac resuscitation if recovery was not possible. "On her last day in the hospital, though, if she took the oxygen away from her nose, she gasped for breath. The doctor offered her a procedure that would make breathing easier, but he warned that there was a possibility she could end up on a ventilator if the procedure didn't work. And incredibly enough, she agreed. A 180-degree turn from what she always said."

"So, what happened, June?" asked Rebecca.

"She passed away before the procedure could take place. I think it was for the best." June's eyes, however, conveyed her lingering sadness.

Cassandra noticed Walter leaning forward as if in thought. "Walter...you looked as if you wanted to say something?"

Walter clasped his hands and shifted in his seat. He seemed uncharacteristically nervous about speaking up. "My mother had heart disease for years," he said in a low, gruff voice. "Dad was busy running the farm, and he looked the other way when my mother was suffering. She wanted to talk about what to do when she got too sick, but he wouldn't. He was such a tough, old codger. Having that talk just doesn't come naturally for some people." He looked down. "It doesn't for me," he said in a softer voice. Walter's heartfelt confession surprised everyone.

The door suddenly blew open, ending the conversation and speculation about this gentler side to Walter's nature.

"So sorry I'm late!" Janie rushed in with a large box of cupcakes she had baked for the evening's treat. "I had to let these cool before frosting them. They're lemon lavender with vanilla icing." She rattled on, barely taking a breath. "Might taste a bit unusual to you. I used real lavender flowers in the mix and decorated them with petals. Looks real purty, as they say back home." When Emma rose to take the box from her, Janie rebuffed her assistance. "Oh, no, don't get up, Emma. I can serve them right from the box."

Taking a cake server from her bag, Janie set a cupcake in front of everyone at the table while George refreshed cups of tea and coffee. The women, in particular, raved about the delicate lemony taste and how pretty the decorations were. Within moments, the little cakes were devoured, and Janie offered a second one to anyone interested. "Emma, do you mind if I stay? I always like to hear what everyone says." With that, she hopped onto the counter and focused intensely on the rest of the discussion. Emma returned to her seat, marveling at how this young woman had always perplexed her.

The meeting ended a short time later. While the attendees wished each other a lovely evening, Walter abruptly got up and, gripping his stomach, ran to the bathroom in the corner of the café. He was evidently unwell since everyone was able to hear him gagging and retching. June turned to see if she could help as Walter stepped out of the bathroom unsteadily. She helped him to a chair, and Emma placed a glass of water and a cold, wet cloth in front of him. June wiped his brow and observed that he had an unfocused, glazed look in his eyes.

"Emma, call emergency. He needs to go to a hospital."

"No, no hospital," Walter croaked. "Just need to rest. I'm... used to this."

"At least let me take you home and call the doctor," Cal said soothingly as he put his arm out to help Walter stand. As Walter tried to get out of the chair, he collapsed against the table, pushing dishes and mugs out of the way, some crashing to the floor. The chair tipped over, and a second later, Walter was on the floor, struggling to breathe. It was evident he was in severe distress.

"Emma, call an ambulance...now!" June took command of the situation.

June knelt at Walter's side. "Everyone, give him room! Move the table, give him some air!" she ordered. Walter was white as a sheet, and sweat glistened on his face. He groaned in agony. Within moments, his body went limp. The former nurse was unable to feel a heartbeat, so she initiated cardiac resuscitation. After several minutes, Rand took over CPR to relieve an exhausted June. He bent low to Walter's nose and could not feel any breath, nor could he feel a heartbeat. Although he continued CPR, he looked at June and shook his head.

Shortly afterward, paramedics arrived and set up their equipment to attempt to revive Walter. The table and chairs were pushed aside to give the men more room. There were shards of mugs and plates and small puddles of coffee and tea on the floor, but this was ignored as eleven horrified people huddled together, watching the scene playing out in front of them. After what seemed like an eternity, the two paramedics sat back from Walter's body on the floor. They had failed to resuscitate their patient, and as they stood, they explained to the shocked group of people what they believed happened. "Possible cardiac arrest, but we won't know till we get him to the ER. There's no heartbeat, but we need to have the doctors at the hospital confirm the death. We're sorry. We did all we could."

The two men lifted Walter's body and placed him on a stretcher, covering him with a sheet. Emma and George accompanied them out to the waiting ambulance. "We'll drive to the hospital as soon as we close up the bookstore," said Emma. "We know you tried everything." George clasped both their hands, wordlessly thanking both men.

Cal and Rebecca offered to drive to Walter's farm and bring Grace to the hospital. "Thank you," Emma said quietly. "We will see you there." She felt drained.

Emma was surprised when Janie offered to stay and clean up. "I'm used to cleaning up messes at the restaurant. If you want to give me your key, I'll lock up and drop off your key tomorrow."

She was too tired to refuse. "Thanks, Janie. That's very kind of you. No hurry, though. We have a spare key at home." Emma turned to her friends, who were trying to restore order in the café. "George and I will call you and let you know what the doctor said. Just...drive carefully, okay?"

Everyone slowly drifted out of the bookstore, reluctant to say goodbye. Cassandra, however, remained in the café.

"I am so sorry this happened," she said to Emma and George. "I just knew that man was a walking time bomb. I thought, though, that it would be Grace on that gurney, not Walter."

Exhausted and wanting to get to the hospital as quickly as possible, Emma simply squeezed Cassandra's hand. "I'll call you in the morning. I can't believe two people have had medical crises in the bookstore—both during your talks. This feels like a nightmare."

With tremendous sorrow for Grace and her children, Emma and George got into their car. In the dark and starless night, they drove in silence to the hospital in Bennington, each with their own thoughts about the death of a complex and difficult man.

chapter twenty-eight
. . .

THE DECISION WAS MADE to close Moose on the Roof Books for the weekend out of respect for the Eammons family. On Sunday morning, Emma, June, and Cassandra met for brunch at a new coffee shop in Bennington. Emma looked forward to being with the two women who had quickly become good friends. She needed to process Friday night's tragic event. After the women were seated at a table cozily set into a deep bay window, Cassandra asked Emma how she felt. Emma looked like she had not slept and was pale as a ghost. "I'm just so stunned about Walter's death. I still can't believe it happened right in front of us! I wonder how Grace is managing."

June let Emma and Cassandra know that Cal and Rebecca have been helping Grace communicate with the hospital and arrange a funeral. The service would be held at Cal's church. Unfortunately, they didn't have a specific date because there may have to be an autopsy. "Cal let me know that the bloodwork showed a toxic amount of digoxin," June said.

"So, that caused his heart to stop so suddenly?" Cassandra asked.

"It appears so," June replied. "I understand that Walter had not been following up with regular blood tests and that particular medication can build up in the blood and become toxic."

"We all know that he drank too much and had anger issues. I guess he was not in good health." Emma took a sip of water. "What stood out for me most before he collapsed, though, was that he actually showed us something real under all that anger and bluster," she said softly. "I've been wondering if it's possible for someone like Walter to change." Emma couldn't help but think how sad his death was if he had made the decision to rehabilitate his behavior. She knew Cal and Rebecca had been counseling him. Perhaps he had begun to understand how his actions had hurt his family and others in the community.

June leaned on her elbows, her chin in her hands, contemplating as she stared out the bay window. When the waitress appeared at their table, the ladies switched gears, briefly focused on the menu, and gave her their orders.

Earlier, George had mentioned to Emma that while she and her friends were in Bennington, he planned to drive to the bookstore to work on repairing the staircase to the belfry. There would be no customers today, so he could work uninterrupted. He had just finished hammering a new stair tread into place when he heard the bell over the front door jingle. He called out, "Who's there? Sorry, but we're closed today!"

Janie appeared in the doorway of Emma's small office. "Hey, George. It's just me. I'm returning the key Emma gave me on Friday night to lock up. Where can I put it?"

"Oh, come on in. I'm fixing the stairs...or trying to, anyway." He laughed as he admitted he was not the handiest guy in the world. "Just hang the key on the hook to the right of the door. And thanks for dropping it off and helping clean up on Friday."

Janie leaned on the corner of Emma's desk, looking up at George. "I bet you and Emma were pretty upset about what happened Friday night. I can't say I'm at all surprised. He hasn't been looking fit lately." She babbled on animatedly about how Grace and her children could now get on with their lives. The workers on the farm loved her and would help her manage for as long as she needed. "Well, I'll be going. I see you have your work cut out for you!"

"Thanks again for closing up Friday night. We'll see you soon." George had been sitting on one of the stairs while visiting with Janie, wondering at her lack of sympathy for Walter's ugly death. She appeared to be in unusually good spirits. As she was about to place the key on the hook, she accidentally dropped it, turned her back to George, and bent down to pick it up. As George looked at her, the memory he had tried to retrieve while on vacation the previous month suddenly clicked into place with a jolt. Frowning, he stood up, murmuring to himself. *It wasn't my sister picking foxglove in the garden*, he thought to himself. *Jenny. Janie. Similar names. And they look enough alike for me to be confused.* "I wasn't hallucinating!" George hadn't realized he had said that last thought out loud.

"Did you say something, George?" asked Janie, aware of George's eyes on her. Suddenly, her expression was flat.

George raised his hand and pointed at Janie. "It was you! You were in my garden one evening picking foxglove. You didn't realize I was looking out the window." He frowned, remembering her behavior one morning at the bookstore. "That's why you acted so strange when you saw the bouquet I brought to the bookstore." He took a shallow breath. "You weren't so sure you hadn't been seen."

Janie's demeanor changed abruptly. Looking intensely at George, she moved a step closer to the stairs. George was beginning to put the pieces together. Nervous now, he backed up one stair. "You know all about herbs and flowers. Did you put something in Walter's cupcake to make him sick? You sure made a big deal about not having anyone help you serve!"

"Look, you have to understand." Janie stood just a few feet from George and raised her hands in supplication. She was a tall, solid woman and seemed to loom over George. He realized she was not denying his accusation.

"Why, Janie? Why would you do such a thing? We saw an innocent man die!" George hoped to keep Janie talking as long as possible. Perhaps Emma or Cal would come in at any moment. Although his eyes kept flitting to the door, he knew he needed to keep them on Janie.

"Innocent?" Janie laughed scornfully and dropped her hands. Her expression became serious, and her eyes locked onto George's. "He ruined his family. I'm glad he's dead."

As the three women waited for their pancakes and omelets at the restaurant, Cassandra said she had something on her mind that had been bothering her since Friday night. "We were all fine after coffee and cake except Walter. I noticed that Janie made a display of explaining what the ingredients were and practically shoved you away, Emma, when you got up to take the box. Something seemed off about that."

June had been gazing out the window deep in thought but suddenly perked up after Cassandra spoke. "I've been thinking, too! When I worked as a nurse, I hardly ever saw someone with digoxin toxicity as young as Walter. It's more common with frailer, older people. Cassandra, do you think Janie added something only to Walter's cupcake? What would...?"

Emma didn't give June a chance to finish her sentence. "Foxglove! It's known as digitalis!" Like George, Emma was also putting the pieces into place. "George saw someone picking foxglove in our back garden. He said it was Jenny, his sister. But it couldn't have been, of course. We all thought he was hallucinating." Emma also remembered an incident shortly after that in the bookstore. "George had brought in a bouquet of foxglove to the shop. When Janie saw it, she acted odd and, again, jabbered away about how dangerous it was to have near customers. After that, I researched it." Emma looked at her friends in horror. "Could she have done something so evil?"

"I say she could." Cassandra was certain. "That nervous chatter of hers. It gives her away."

"Hold on, I'm getting a text," said Emma. "Maybe it's George." Scrolling to the message, Emma rose to her feet quickly, her chair almost tipping over. "It was Janie. She's returning the key to the bookstore now. June, George is there by himself. We have to go now!"

"Go!" said Cassandra. "I'll get the check. Be careful! And hurry!"

George backed up another couple of steps. His balance faltered on one of the treads, and as he grabbed the handrail, the hammer he had been using slipped out of his hand and clattered to the floor. His heart thudded in his chest. George looked at Janie and saw her eyes flicker with fear and uncertainty. He hoped he could use that uncertainty to his advantage.

Projecting an air of bravery, Janie jutted her chin out. "I had to do it. My father slapped my mother around when he got drunk. He didn't stop until my mom...well, that doesn't matter anymore." She took a ragged breath." Walter wouldn't have stopped either, not till he killed Grace. And Jesse...that sweet boy. Walter would have turned him into someone mean and distrustful. Jesse hated his father. Do you think he would have ever been safe with Walter?"

With every word, Janie became more disturbed. "I'm begging you to keep this between us. Don't you see? Everyone is better off without him. Please! I can't give up my life with Mike. He means everything to me."

George realized Janie was wavering between begging George to keep her secret and figuring out how to silence him. He had talked down people who were agitated and in crisis before. "Janie, I was a cop. I'm sure I can figure out something to help you. Let's go into the café, have a cup of tea, and calm down. We'll call Cal, and together, we'll work this out. I'd like to know about your parents." George wanted to keep her talking. She seemed to be equating her family and Grace's, as if she was experiencing PTSD.

"No! You're just trying to trick me. They'll arrest me. Just like my mother." At this revelation, Janie seemed to have made her decision and boldly moved closer to George. Frightened and understanding that Janie was becoming manic, George backed up the remainder of the steep, winding steps into the belfry. He looked around the small tower and saw nothing to grab as a weapon. He realized how vulnerable he was.

Janie was young and strong. A second later, she appeared at the top of the staircase. She took one more step and stood, breathless and desperate, facing George.

Janie glanced around the small space, barely large enough for two people. She looked over the low wall to the ground far below. It was another sweltering August morning, made even more oppressive by fear and the nearness of their two bodies. Although tears ran down Janie's face, George saw purpose in her expression as she edged closer. Her eyes were cold and focused. George understood she was counting on his lack of balance to solve her dilemma.

"Janie..." George rasped. His throat was so dry. His fear and the oppressive heat made him feel faint. He reached out, trying to hold onto something...praying desperately...when he realized that the rope to ring the bell was right in front of him. He wrapped his arms tightly around it and pulled with every fiber of his being, hoping someone would wonder why a bell that hadn't been rung in years was now ringing. George cried with joy when the bell pealed resoundingly.

The crows, who were roosting on the tower's exposed rafters, were startled and reacted immediately to the disruption. Squawking and flying helter-skelter around the cramped belfry, the birds distracted Janie. She lifted her arms to shield her face and inadvertently stepped back to avoid them. Too late, she realized with horror that the tower's knee-high wall was behind her, and she stumbled. With frightened eyes, she implored George to help her.

Still clutching the rope, George leaned forward. "Janie! Grab my hand!" George immediately responded to save her life, no matter what transpired between them.

Janie reached for George's outstretched hand, but the momentum had carried her too far over the edge. George's hand grasped only air. Seconds after her scream, he heard the thud of her body landing on the ground below. It seemed that time had stopped.

By the time George recovered his breath and looked down, Janie's body had come to rest in the small church graveyard. Her head had smashed against one of the old gravestones, and her legs jutted out at awkward angles. Blood...so much blood...was already pooling around her broken body.

chapter twenty-nine
. . .

"GEORGE!" was all Emma could say through her tears. She and June had driven like wildfire to Mill River and parked June's car as close to Moose on The Roof Books as possible. To Emma, it seemed as if all she saw were flashing red lights, police, and medical personnel swarming around the bookstore. She had begun to panic before finally spotting her husband sitting on the rear running board of the ambulance, wrapped in a blanket the paramedics provided. George held a hot cup of coffee Rebecca had brought over for him. Emma saw Caleb talking and gesturing to two police officers.

"I'd never heard that bell ring before and was curious what was happening, so I looked out my office window," Cal said. "I saw Janie and George on the belfry, and just as Janie seemed to lose her balance, George reached for her, but she stumbled over the side. I saw crows flying like bats out of Hell. I can only think they must have scared Janie." Cal continued after a momentary pause so that he could regain his composure. "I ran over, but of course, it was too late. Janie's head struck...well, you saw. I told Rebecca to call you and then ran up to help George."

Caleb had cautiously walked up the rickety steps to the bell tower and discovered a distraught George still gripping the rope, sobbing in horror and relief. He coaxed George down the staircase, carefully supporting his friend. "By that time..." Caleb explained, "...the ambulance had arrived, and the paramedics were ready to take over. The police got here a few minutes later."

"Mrs. Nielsen?" a young female police officer approached Emma. "Do you think your husband can answer a few questions?" Emma looked at George, but it was apparent he was still in shock. He was shivering, and tears were still pooling in his eyes. Paramedics found that he was physically unhurt, but after his encounter in the belfry, he was emotionally overwrought.

"I think your questions may have to wait, Officer," Emma spoke gently.

"Of course. We'll check in with you tomorrow."

Emma thanked her and, noticing that the team from the morgue was about to remove Janie's body, hugged her husband closely so that he would not have to witness their work. The men enclosed the body in a black shroud and placed her in the waiting ambulance. Emma shuddered when she heard them slowly zip the bag. She closed her eyes and prayed for Janie's soul. And she said a heartfelt prayer of gratitude that George was safe.

The police detective in charge of the investigation cleared George to go home. Since he was still examining the office and belfry, Emma gave him the extra key she always carried.

Cal and Rebecca came to sit with Emma and George for a few minutes. "Cal, how can I ever thank you? You and Rebecca are true friends."

"No thanks needed," Cal said. "Why don't you two head home now. You both need something to eat and to rest. I'll see you tomorrow." He tenderly laid his hand on George's shoulder.

Emma pecked him on the cheek. George looked up through red-rimmed eyes and nodded his thanks. Ignoring the onlookers who always seemed to assemble for a tragedy, Emma bundled George into June's car for the ride home. If she had looked back, she would have seen Mike racing frantically toward the bookstore, collapsing when he reached the ambulance carrying his wife.

Once they reached their beloved cottage, Emma hugged June hard and whispered a thank you. "Don't worry about your car, Emma. Rob and I will bring it to you tomorrow. Now, go take care of your husband."

Emma cradled George's hand in her own and led him to the front door. George sat down wordlessly on the sofa and closed his eyes. "Would you like something to eat?" she asked. "I can make oatmeal or scrambled eggs, something comforting?"

"No, thank you, though, Em. I think I just want to sleep."

And that he did, immediately. Emma placed a soft blanket over him and kissed his forehead. Sensing an opportunity for a warm nap, Annie leaped onto the sofa and cuddled into the crook of George's knees. Emma called Maggie and Jack to let them know what happened. She asked Maggie to contact Jennifer as well. She made tea, toasted an English muffin, and then ate at the kitchen table, thinking of Mike and Ronnie. "They must be devastated," she said softly to herself.

Emma still didn't know what had happened between her husband and Janie and did not want to push George for details. Caleb had told Emma that George kept repeating: "It was foxglove. Janie picked the foxglove." Emma surmised that Janie somehow came to the conclusion that George suspected her of poisoning Walter's cupcake. She hoped a good rest would help George remember what happened on that bell tower.

Over the next several days, the police detective questioned George, Caleb, and Janie's husband and mother-in-law. Mill River is a small town, and most people either know or know of everyone else. And Mike and Janie were well-liked. So, the detective and police officers sympathized with Janie's family when they had to inform them that the search of his house and barn had yielded evidence of malicious intentions. They found tiny particles of foxglove root and leaves in the pipes under the sink in the barn.

Walter's autopsy had revealed an overdose of digoxin in his body, far more than the amount prescribed by the dead man's physician. His death was declared a homicide; however, the alleged perpetrator was now dead as well. The investigation cleared George of any wrongdoing in Janie's death, and the case was closed. Emma realized that Janie's offer of help the evening Walter died was born out of a desire to eliminate any evidence that would implicate her.

Emma stayed home with George for two weeks and was heartened to see her husband gradually returning to himself. He was able to talk more openly about his sadness and guilt in not being able to reach Janie's hand.

"But she was threatening you on the stairs. What did you think she was going to do?" Emma fought to control her emotions.

"I honestly don't know, Emma. Her expression wavered between frightened and, yes, threatening. I was afraid, and yet…

I think she was figuring out what to do minute by minute. I think she might have thought I would simply lose my balance. She knew about the Parkinson's." A look of horror clouded George's face, and he shuddered. "Those damned birds were flying every which way. They startled her, ...and I can't stop seeing her face as she went over." George covered his face with his hands and wept.

During her time away from the bookstore, Emma did everything she knew to make her husband comfortable. They took walks on the trails near their cottage. She cooked simple meals of soups, crusty bread, and cheese from a local dairy. They binged hours of movies and television shows. Every night, they took a glass of wine or a cup of tea onto the patio and watched the evening sky turn teal, pink, and finally midnight blue, punctuated by stars.

Eventually, however, Emma felt she had to open the bookstore for a few hours each day. Whenever they could, June and Cassandra stopped by and sat in the café with Emma, listening to her worries about George, her concern for Grace and her children, and Mike and Ronnie. Caleb took George out for coffee or lunch, and Caleb and Rebecca came to the cottage for dinner at least once weekly.

Maggie and Jack arrived the second weekend. "Daddy," Maggie cried as she hugged her father tightly.

"Dad," said Jack solemnly. Jack held his emotions in check, but the worry in his eyes showed his concern for his father. The children wanted to know exactly what happened in the bell tower, and George accommodated them but tried to downplay how truly frightened he was.

"Mom," scolded Maggie as she marched into the kitchen.

"What are you going to do now? You can't possibly be serious about keeping that store! Dad almost died!"

Emma looked at her daughter and could see the concern etched on the younger woman's lovely face. "Sit down, sweetheart. Dad and I will figure out what to do. I haven't even wanted to discuss the future of The Moose yet."

Maggie smiled when she heard her mother's nickname for the bookstore. "Okay, I understand, but I'm not sure Dad will ever want to set foot in that place again. He's broken up about Janie."

"I know he is. Don't forget, though, that she took it upon herself to poison Walter. Whether she meant to kill him or hurt him, I don't know. And I don't know what she would have done to your father if things had turned out differently."

As she gazed out the French doors to the garden beyond, Maggie seemed lost in thought. She slowly nodded her head in agreement. "Is it awful, Mom, if I thank God it wasn't Dad who fell?"

The following week, while Emma was tidying up the shelves in the store, she was surprised when Ronnie appeared, standing hesitantly at the front door. "Hi, Emma," she said softly, not knowing if she would be welcome.

"Oh, Ronnie. I...I don't know what to say. I can't imagine how sad you are." Emma wasn't sure whether to stand where she was or to hug Janie's mother-in-law.

Fortunately, Ronnie made the first move and tentatively walked toward Emma. "Can we talk, Emma? Do you have a few minutes?"

"Of course. How about a cup of coffee? I'll bring it out here, and we'll sit by the coffee table. These armchairs are so comfortable." Emma knew she was rambling, but she didn't want Ronnie to come into the café where Walter had died. She brought out two steaming mugs of coffee from the pot she had just brewed and sat in the chair facing Ronnie. "Please tell me how you and Mike are managing. Is Mike taking a break from the restaurant?"

"He drove to West Virginia to see Janie's family," Ronnie said. "Her mother still lives in the little town where Janie grew up. And there's an aunt and a couple of cousins." Ronnie fidgeted with a ring on her hand. "Emma, what Janie did was unforgivable, and I am so sorry. I pray every night that George will recover from…well, what Janie put him through."

"He is beginning to get better, Ronnie. Thank you for caring. I'm sure it wasn't easy for you to come here."

"I didn't know if you would even let me in the bookstore." Ronnie peered at Emma through watery eyes.

Emma handed Ronnie a tissue and moved her chair closer to the other woman. Leaning forward, she took both of Ronnie's hands in hers. "Neither you nor Mike have anything to apologize for. Janie acted on her own. If it's any consolation, George is miserable that he could not save her. Despite her intentions."

Ronnie sipped her coffee and wiped her eyes with the tissue. She nodded her head in gratitude and took a deep breath. "Maybe I should keep quiet, but I wanted to tell you a little about Janie's history. It won't change anything, but I guess I'm trying to make sense of her thinking, too." Ronnie paused a moment, collecting herself. "Would you mind if I shared it with you?"

All Emma could do was nod her silent assent.

Focusing on the hands she had folded on her lap, Ronnie

smiled sadly. "Janie's not...was not...a bad person. She had her demons, though. I think watching Walter abuse Grace was a trigger for her. She grew up with her father pushing and slapping her mother. And just like Walter, he was cunning. He never used his fists, never broke any bones. Clothes usually hid any bruises he made. He was an angry and bitter man who felt the world owed him more than a job on a work crew and a wife who was just a small-town diner waitress. Also, like Walter, drinking just made his mood uglier."

Ronnie stopped abruptly, considering how to continue. "Well...I guess you should know that Janie's mother finally fought back. During one of his drunken rages, she took a baseball bat to his legs. Janie was hiding under the bed but saw the horrible fight. Her father wouldn't press charges because the whole sordid story would come out. He eventually left town. Stayed away for good. Janie's grandmother took on the role of her protector. She'd take Janie to her cabin, feed her, sew her clothes, and spend time in the woods teaching her how to forage. Althea was one of those old, independent mountain women. Janie adored her." Ronnie smiled as she thought about the close relationship Janie had described.

"Janie was so fortunate to have her in her life. It sounds like Janie took on the same role for Grace."

"And the kids, too. She had a special bond with Jesse. Janie fretted about Grace's safety constantly. Just couldn't let it go. She felt that someday Walter would go too far and kill Grace. She never got past the abuse she grew up with. Even after she married Mike and she was safe and loved."

"So, she hatched some kind of plan to poison Walter...here, in our bookstore? We know she took the foxglove from our garden. It was growing like a weed in the backyard."

Ronnie sighed deeply. "This is, unfortunately, where you and George come in. Janie had a distorted idea that your café was robbing the restaurant of customers. I believe that somehow, she felt if someone died during that program about death, that people would be spooked and stop shopping here. It never sat right with me that Janie was too interested in what happened to that poor librarian who had gone to the hospital after drinking herbal tea during one of those evenings." Seemingly drained from relating her story, Ronnie sank back in her chair and waited for a response from Emma.

"Oh, that is so twisted, and sad, and so wrong. How could we ever take business away from your restaurant? Why did she agree to bake for us? And Walter! Do you honestly think she meant to kill him? She couldn't be sure of that." Emma was perplexed.

"I truly wish I knew the answers to those questions. I know she told Mike that baking for you was helping Moose on the Roof attract her customers. And yet, it brought in extra cash. Janie was obsessed with having enough money. I guess I just wanted to tell you how sorry I am and to maybe explain Janie's thinking. I truly hope that George will be all right."

"He is getting better, Ronnie. I can't tell you what our future holds. George and I are skirting around the subject of the bookstore right now."

Ronnie stood up and looked at Grace with a sad smile. "Whatever you and George decide to do, please know I wish you the best. You've both been wonderful for our community. I'm glad you're here." She gently took Emma's hands in hers in a gesture of farewell and left as quietly as she came in.

chapter thirty

...

AFTER EMMA CLOSED UP shop a short time later, she hopped into her car, waved at Cal, who was deep in conversation with one of his parishioners in front of his church and headed home. She decided to stop at the take-out place for a roasted eggplant and mozzarella hero and side salad for a quick dinner. The weather was perfect, and Emma took her time on the country road. She was grateful for Ronnie's visit but decided not to tell George about it.

Her mind was occupied with other concerns. It was the end of the summer season and the fields of corn were now full of dry brown stalks, beautiful in their austerity. Farmstands were beginning to sell wreaths made of corn husks and bittersweet. Varieties of sweet-eating apples and tart apples for baking began appearing in baskets in front of farmstands. Finally, Emma made the right turn into her long gravel driveway, maple trees just at the precipice of autumn color, forming a graceful archway as she approached the cottage.

"Hey, George. I'm home!" Emma called as she walked through the front door. "I brought dinner. Can you help me bring the plates and silverware out back?" They often dined on the patio in the backyard.

"Coming," George replied from the den. I've got to get Annie off me first. Shake the bag of dry food, okay?"

Emma heard four feet land on the floor and scurry to the kitchen. George ambled in after her, kissed Emma, and dutifully set the picnic table.

Once they were seated, Emma served up the hero and salad. After she took a sip of wine, Emma leaned forward and looked resolutely at her husband. She did not want to beat around the bush anymore. "George, I think we need to talk about the bookstore. I want to know if you can feel comfortable working there again."

"Honestly, I don't know, dear. My stomach feels queasy when I think of returning. We've had a wonderful year and met some great people because of the bookstore, but being retired is becoming more appealing." George stretched out his legs. "Before these old legs stiffen up and I have more difficulty walking, I'd like to travel more. How many more years will we be able to do that? But having said that, I know The Moose was your dream. I feel you should decide its future."

"Thank you for being honest. There's that part of me that always thinks that things will turn out all right. I'm not always logical, I know. So, let me think about it. I know what our kids would want. Probably for us to sit on the couch, you reading a book and me knitting endless afghans for Annie for the rest of our days. And I don't even knit!" Emma laughed as she remembered so many conversations with her unattached kids. "But I'd learn to knit in a second if we had grandchildren."

Two months later, Maggie came up behind Emma. "Hey, Mom. Are you almost ready?"

Emma turned from the window, looking out at the autumn garden. "In a couple of minutes," she said, smiling at her daughter. I want to thank you and Jack for ripping out that awful bed of foxglove. Good riddance! I'm thinking a pretty snowball hydrangea would fit quite nicely in that spot next spring."

Maggie joined her mother at the window, casually throwing her arm over Emma's shoulder. "I agree, and we'll be here to help you. So, we're all in the kitchen and ready when you are."

After Maggie left the bedroom, Emma stood in front of the mirror. Sighing deeply, Emma once again considered her image. "My goodness," she thought. "One year has gone by. A year older, a little grayer, hopefully a bit wiser." She recalled the conversation she and George had in early September as they sat on their patio. A few days later, she presented what she thought would be a perfect plan. Yes, it was time to enjoy life without the stress of business ownership, and she understood that her husband would always have misgivings about continuing with the bookstore.

They agreed to sell Moose on the Roof, at a significantly reduced amount, to the Town of Mill River, specifically for a new, expanded library. Their proposal was greeted enthusiastically by the town and the library staff. As Emma returned her thoughts to the present, she wound a tartan wool scarf that complimented her dark blue pantsuit around her shoulders. One more look, and Emma was ready to join her family in the kitchen. "Show time," she told herself, discovering she was genuinely looking forward to the day's festivities.

"Finally!" said George with a wink. After everyone piled into the car, George started the engine and looked at Emma, his eyebrows raised comically. "So, we're off like a herd of turtles," he said, puffing away on a pretend cigar in a poor imitation of Groucho Marx. This never failed to get an eye roll from Emma. Secretly, she was relieved his sense of humor, however awful, had returned along with a renewed sense of well-being.

As they parked on Main Street, Emma took note of the group of people gathering on the sidewalk. She saw Ed, the sign maker, who had once again been called upon for his expertise. Emma and her family joined the group just as the president of the library's board of directors signaled that the ceremony would now begin. After a brief speech, Ed was directed to pull the tarp. Emma was overwhelmed when she read the sign: The Moose on the Roof Memorial Library. George pulled Emma close while she swiped at her teary eyes.

After the ceremony in front of the new library, the group moved inside for champagne toasts and canapés. In addition to the librarians and a few town officials, several of the Nielsen's friends had been invited. Emma took George's hand as he took a hesitant step into the old church. Fortunately, he found that the library evoked only good memories of the bookstore. He smiled back at Emma and walked with ease into the celebration.

As George was swallowed up in their crowd of friends, Emma took a glass of champagne and observed from a corner of the library. Cal had corralled her children and Jennifer into an animated conversation. She saw Cassandra introduce her very handsome husband to Rob Jamieson, who had also worked as a professor at Bennington College. June was busy ensuring everyone had a plate of the delicious food the Inn had provided. Rebecca stood beside Grace, who was shyly looking around at the guests mingling. Following her line of sight, Emma was not surprised to see Rand meeting her gaze from the other side of the room, a sweet grin on his face. Emma did not see Roger among the attendees. She missed the pharmacist, who spent more and more time at his mountain cabin.

Emma extricated herself from the party and slipped into her old office, now furnished for its new occupant, Marie, the new library administrator. Her eyes were drawn to the staircase to the bell tower. Contractors had been hired to redo the stairs entirely, and they were now solid and safe. Emma rested her hand on the finial at the bottom of the flight of steps and peered toward the tower. She decided to take one more look at the town from the top of the church and climbed carefully up to the belfry.

Her stomach lurched as she thought of George and Janie facing one another in this small space. The contractors, however, had wisely added a safety rail to the knee-high wall. Emma leaned on one of the rails and remembered how she stood up here a little over a year ago to admire the quaint town and the farmland spread out like a patchwork quilt beneath her. This time, there was heartache as she thought about the losses this town had sustained. Remembering Janie, she quietly prayed as she looked down at the small graveyard behind the old church. Both Walter and Janie had been laid to rest in the cemetery just north of Mill River.

Emma heard footsteps on the stairs behind her. Her heart quickened until she saw who it was. She smiled fondly as Cal ascended the final step. "Saying goodbye, Emma?"

"Reminiscing. What a year it's been since I met you on that first day. You, with your exorcist suit and stories about a murder of crows!" The corner of Emma's eyes crinkled as she recalled that October morning.

Cal waggled his eyebrows and laughed in remembrance.

Emma turned serious. "I want to understand how George felt up here with Janie. What do you think really happened, Cal?"

"Fight or flight. Janie was faced with the truth of what she had done to Walter and had to choose. Would she have pushed George? We'll never know. It's possible she thought his unsteadiness would solve the problem for her."

"Yes, that's certainly possible," Emma mused. "Cal, have I told you enough how much I appreciate you for responding so quickly and helping George get down the stairs to safety?"

"You have. And I'm so glad I heard that bell." After a beat, Cal shook his head, reflecting. "Even after everything I see as a minister, it's still hard to digest the circumstances that led to Walter's and Janie's deaths. Walter was an abusive husband and father. Janie wanted to protect Grace and her children, but that desire led to tragedy." Cal gazed off into the distance, contemplating for a couple of minutes. "But now you and George have given the community a wonderful gift. A library they can be proud of." He turned to Emma with the old twinkle in his eyes. "And you know, those crows are the real heroes here. I told you from that first day they're smart and loyal."

"You have a weird sense of humor, Caleb Hill. But I can't disagree." As Cal descended the stairs, Emma glanced down at the graveyard and offered a silent word of gratitude to the crows pecking obliviously among the juniper bushes. She took a deep breath and discovered she was ready to return to the party and the beginning of a new chapter in her life.

chapter thirty-one
. . .

EMMA'S BUDDY, ROGER, HAD decided to skip the dedication of the new library. Most of his days now were spent at his log cabin by a lake deep in the woods in the Green Mountain National Park. This relaxed November afternoon, he was ensconced in a comfortable armchair reading the latest bestseller on a presidential scandal. The cabin's wood stove cast warmth and a cozy glow in the dim afternoon sun. Roger's old dog, Charlie, was by his side, his legs twitching as he dreamed.

Roger looked up as he heard a knock on the window and saw Lauren's smiling face peering in at him. He waved her in, and she came through the door, bringing the cinnamon scent of freshly baked crumb cake with her.

"This is a nice surprise. Pull up a seat. Want some coffee? There's some in the pot."

"Don't get up. I'll pour." After filling her cup and replenishing Roger's, Lauren sat in the rocking chair opposite her father. She set the cake on the coffee table and sliced a piece for both of them. Lauren looked at her father's face as Roger reached for his plate. Spending time in the mountains with his dog and books had relaxed his features. She hated to disturb his peace.

Lauren took a sip of coffee. She wished she had a shot of some liquid courage to bolster what she had to say.

"Dad," Lauren reached out to take one of Roger's hands into her own. She looked into his eyes. "I know your secret," her voice hardly above a whisper.

"I'm sorry, but I'm not sure what you mean." Roger disengaged his hand and sank back into his recliner, crossing his legs. Lauren noticed a tic under his right eye that belied his casual pose.

She leaned closer to her dad. "You switched medications with Walter. The investigators came to the pharmacy after talking with Walter's doctor. His medication orders all checked out, but I just had this feeling something didn't add up. I found your medication vials on one of the days you were home. I know the code on the pills, Dad. You were taking a lesser dosage of digoxin than your doctor prescribed. You'd been putting your pills in Walter's pill vials. That's why he had such a high level of toxicity in his blood. And why you have been more tired and short of breath. It's just taken me a while to figure out what to say to you."

Roger looked outside at the gray clouds heralding snow as they began to coalesce. He could not meet his daughter's eyes. Surprised and somewhat off-kilter by Lauren's revelation, he could not formulate a response.

"Dad, I understand!" Lauren put her hand over her heart. "What Walter and his friends did to me has eaten away at you for years. The last few months seem to have made his verbal attacks worse. Unfortunately, it's been difficult to avoid him at Cassandra's meetings. My God, this summer, he just seemed to be everywhere." Lauren took a sip of coffee and continued when Roger maintained his silence. "You blamed Walter for taking away the life you think I should have rightfully had. A husband. A home. Family. But lately, I've realized that I have most of those things. I have you...my daughter...a couple of good friends who care about me, not what I look like." She held her fingers to the scar that marred her otherwise pretty face. "It may not be the life everyone would want, but it's mine, and I'm grateful for it." Lauren's eyes filled with tears. "I'll keep your secret, Dad. It's my turn to protect you."

Roger leaned forward, his elbows on his jean-clad knees. He cupped his face in his hands, and when he looked up at Lauren, there was relief in his eyes, his burden of secrecy lifted. "Oh, my dear Lauren, you have been a blessing to me and your mother, always and forever." Roger's voice was husky with emotion. "I'm so sorry I put you in the middle of this. I forgot how smart you are!" Lauren reached out, once again reaching for her father's hands, as Roger composed himself.

"And I'm sorry, too, about Janie," he said. "Not that she was innocent of intent, but I know the amount of foxglove in that cupcake could never have killed Walter. On top of the increased dose and his terrible health, it just put his heart over the edge." Gazing out the window, he now noticed a few snowflakes starting to fall. Roger's heart was heavy, matching the darkening afternoon. "I don't know how to face Emma and George. I feel awful that Walter died in front of everyone that night. And poor George. I can't imagine how frightened he must have been on that belfry."

Lauren just nodded sadly, knowing how much he cared about the Nielsens. "Dad, did you know that Emma and George have sold the bookstore, and the library was dedicated today?"

"That's the reason I'm here. I feel so guilty that their lives have changed because of something I did." He looked at Lauren unflinchingly. "I don't regret that Walter is gone, though. He put his family...and you...through so much heartache."

"Everyone seems to be okay. I've seen Grace, and Jesse hanging out with his friends in town. Emma has visited the pharmacy asking about you. She misses seeing you." Looking around the cabin, Lauren realized her father had everything he needed there. "So, it looks like you're pretty set. You won't be moving back to the house?"

"No, I'm ready for some peace and quiet out here in the woods. But I'll be coming into town, and we'll visit often. I'm content that the pharmacy is in good hands with you and Katie. You'll both be here for Thanksgiving?"

"Of course." Lauren rose and took the dishes to the cottage sink. "Come on. Get that lazy old dog up and walk me to my car."

Lauren was parked at the head of the trail leading to the cabin. Father and daughter walked in silence, enjoying the sound of leaves crunching underfoot. A fawn scooted across the trail, followed by its graceful mother, who shot a curious look at the couple. She twitched her tail and disappeared through the trees.

At Lauren's car, she hugged her dad tightly and kissed him on the cheek. "I love you too, Dad. Always and forever," echoing Roger's earlier sentiment. Roger and Charlie stood side by side, watching Lauren as she put the car into gear and backed out of the small clearing. He didn't see his daughter glance back in the rearview mirror and whisper, "Thank you, Dad. You'll always be my hero." She acknowledged, however, that her father's actions led to the loss of two lives.

Lauren picked up speed as she entered the highway and drove back through the gathering dusk to Mill River. Lauren looked once again in the mirror. She saw that her eyes were crinkled in genuine happiness, and there was a feeling in her heart she was not used to. It was hope.

epilogue

...

AS LAUREN WAS ON her way to Mill River, Emma and her family drove toward Benny's Pizza Restaurant, one of their favorite restaurants in Manchester, for dinner after the library's dedication party. Once inside, they ordered pizza, calzones, and a large Greek salad. Jennifer raided the refrigerator and brought mini bottles of red wine to the table. "My treat! Who wants to make a toast?"

"I will," George said, raising his glass. "To Moose on the Roof Memorial Library and retirement!"

"To good food," Jack added, taking a whiff of the fragrant pizza the waitress had just served. "Oh, that is perfect!"

"So," Maggie asked her parents, "What will you do now that you're officially retired?"

"I have about a hundred books I've been meaning to read. I want to plan my spring garden. Dr Shah wants me to start physical therapy to strengthen my legs. And Annie and I will enjoy some time on the couch together. I think retirement will agree with me." George leaned back in his chair with a contented smile on his face.

"Mom? You're ignoring my question."

"Not really, honey. I'll take a few weeks to recoup, but I've been missing my old job. A small nursing home about twenty minutes from home is looking for volunteers. Maybe just one or two days a week. I need to have some purpose. Would that be okay with you, George?"

"You mean I won't have you asking me to do chores on those days? Then it's fine with me!"

Emma applied for and was accepted as a volunteer at Willow Hill Nursing Home and Rehabilitation Center. George requested physical therapy for the two days Emma worked. Emma, June, and Cassandra looked forward to continuing their friendship. They planned lunches together and dinners in each other's homes as often as possible and intended to bring Cal and Rebecca into their fellowship. Once the library's programs were developed, the librarians asked Emma to read to the younger children occasionally.

When Emma needed prescriptions filled, she spent a few minutes chatting with Katie and Lauren. Lauren no longer hid behind her computer. Emma noticed a new-found optimism, which translated to a new hairstyle and an updated wardrobe. Lauren confided that she even consulted with a plastic surgeon in Burlington. Emma did miss Roger, who appeared to be permanently ensconced in his mountain cabin with his sidekick pooch, Charlie.

Cal told Emma that Grace and Rand had begun attending church together Sunday morning. Some parishioners reported seeing them holding hands in the pew. The small town's gossip mill was in full swing. Emma was hopeful they would find the happiness in love that had eluded them and that

Grace's children would feel safe and protected.

Mike brought Janie's mother to Vermont to attend a private funeral for her daughter. He was not surprised when he heard a door open at the back of the funeral home and saw Grace quietly slip into a chair. She was gone before the service ended. Mike thought he would take a few weeks off. He found, however, that he could channel his grief into chopping, slicing, and stirring the ingredients for meals for his faithful customers. He returned to The Down Home Grill after Janie's funeral. The town stood by both Mike and Grace.

On a chilly Sunday afternoon, when the library was closed, Emma stood gazing up at the building. She reflected on all the events of the past year. She was saddened by the tragic loss of two townspeople and by the loss of her dream. Emma couldn't help being optimistic, though. She loved her charming Vermont town and the friends she and George had made. Her husband was safe, and she was looking forward to her volunteer work. Emma left her old bookstore with those thoughts in mind. Her final task was to place a stone marker where Janie had fallen. Janie had wanted to save the friend she loved, but would she have sacrificed George to keep her secret? Emma would never know, so she quietly said a prayer for this tragically flawed young woman.

As Emma left the graveyard, she saw the crows again lined up on the steeple as if for evening Taps. They were staring down at her inquisitively. She pulled the bag of breadcrumbs from her coat pocket and scattered them by the juniper bushes. "Caleb told me you guys were loyal," she said hushedly to the mysterious birds. "Do you know that you saved my husband? Thank you, my friends." Emma waved goodbye and, on her way out of the garden, saw a pile of shiny bottle caps on a stone pillar. Laughing, she looked again at the birds, now swooping down for their treat. She scooped up their gifts, laid her hand once more on Janie's marker, and walked out of the graveyard toward her jeep.

One morning, shortly before Christmas, Emma got ready for her first day at the nursing home. She wore her best jeans, a festive red turtleneck sweater, and warm boots. She placed her locket containing childhood photos of Maggie and Jack around her neck. The cottage was decorated for Christmas, and the tree they brought home sent waves of fragrant pine through the rooms. A light snow had fallen during the night, and the trees and lawn were dusted with sparkling new snow. Emma bundled up in her parka, wool scarf, and gloves.

"George, I'm set to leave," she called. "There's soup in the fridge and biscuits in the bread box. I'll see you about three." George ambled in from the den, anticipating a day of reading and practicing being a couch potato. Emma's eyes were wide and full of anticipation. "I'm really looking forward to volunteering at Willow Hill. It's like a new adventure!" She kissed George and fairly ran to her car.

George looked out the window until Emma's taillights were no longer visible. Annie stood next to him, gazing up with her wise, green eyes, whiskers twitching and ears rotating like radar. "Hmmm. You felt it, too?" He leaned down to stroke the cat's long, soft fur. He gave out a theatrical sigh. "That's exactly what she said when we bought the bookstore!"

THE END

acknowledgments

As always, I owe a huge note of appreciation to my family for believing in me. Thank you to editor Stacey Goitia and artist Gareth Southwell from Reedsy. You both went beyond my expectations. And finally, I am so glad for the friendship I have found in the Cutchogue Writer's Group. I appreciate your careful reading and thoughtful suggestions.

about the author

Bonnie Stock is the author of *Your Third Act: Navigating Life in an Adult Care Community*. She brings her love of Vermont to life in this light mystery about love, revenge, and family in a small community. She and her husband had enjoyed a second home in Vermont for many years, and the inspiration for this story is drawn from the beauty and intrigue of the state. Bonnie and her husband live on the North Fork of Long Island with their sweet tuxedo cat, Maggie May. Join her on Facebook at Moose on the Roof Books for an update on the next mystery series book.

Made in the USA
Middletown, DE
03 November 2024